YORK NOTES

General Editors: Professor A.N. Jeffares (*University of Stirling*) & Professor Suheil Bushrui (*American University of Beirut*)

William Faulkner

THE SOUND AND THE FURY

Notes by C.E. Nicholson

BA (LEEDS), *Lecturer in English and American Literature, University of Edinburgh*

and *Randall Stevenson*

MA (EDINBURGH), M LITT (OXFORD), *Lecturer in English Literature, University of Edinburgh*

 LONGMAN
YORK PRESS

YORK PRESS
Immeuble Esseily, Place Riad Solh, Beirut.

LONGMAN GROUP UK LIMITED
Longman House, Burnt Mill, Harlow,
Essex CM20 2JE, England
and Associated Companies throughout the world.

First published 1981
Fourth impression 1993

ISBN 0582 78195 7

Produced by Longman Singapore Publishers Pte Ltd
Printed in Singapore

Contents

Part 1
Introduction

The life of William Faulkner

William Falkner was born on 25 September 1897 in New Albany, Mississippi, moving in 1901 to Oxford, Mississippi. There his father, Murray Charles Falkner, operated a livery stable and then ran a hardware store before becoming business manager of the University of Mississippi. Falkner did not attend school regularly, and he left, without graduating, to work in his grandfather's bank. In 1918 he served briefly with the Royal Canadian Flying Corps where he was in training when the First World War ended. After the war he returned to Oxford and was enrolled as a special student at the University of Mississippi. He did well in French and Spanish but was awarded the grades of D and F for his studies in English. It was also during these years as a student, between 1919 and 1921, that he began to use the name Faulkner rather than Falkner when he wrote sketches for the campus newspaper *The Mississippian*.

At the invitation of the writer and critic Stark Young, Faulkner made his first trip to New York in 1920, where he worked in a bookshop managed by Elizabeth Sprall, who later married the novelist Sherwood Anderson (1876–1941). He returned to Oxford to become postmaster at the University of Mississippi, a job he held until his resignation in 1924. He had been slipshod as postmaster, spending too much of his time reading and writing. But in the year of his resignation, Faulkner's first book, a collection of poems called *The Marble Faun,* was published. Although these early attempts at poetry were not successful, Faulkner was to persist in his efforts at verse. He published a second and equally unsuccessful volume of poems, *The Green Bough*, in 1933. In later life he liked to refer to himself as a failed poet who had turned to prose fiction as 'the next best thing'.

Early in 1925 Faulkner went to New Orleans, intending to sail from there to Europe. But no place was available on a ship and he stayed in New Orleans for six months. Here he first met Sherwood Anderson, already well known since the publication of *Winesburg, Ohio* (1919). Anderson was to offer him decisive help and encouragement. Faulkner published poems, sketches, and essays in the New Orleans *Times-Picayune* and in the literary magazine *The Double Dealer*. He also collaborated with the artist William Spratling on a book called

Sherwood Anderson and other Creoles (1926) which parodied Anderson's style and so cost Faulkner the friendship of the older writer. During six weeks of his stay in New Orleans, Faulkner wrote his first novel, *Soldier's Pay*, which was eventually published in 1926. In 1925, he sailed off on his long-delayed trip to Europe, working his passage in the engine room and on deck. He roamed around northern Italy by bicycle and on foot before travelling to France to settle for a short time in the Latin Quarter of Paris. Later he said about this part of his trip, 'I knew Joyce, I knew of Joyce, and I would go to some effort to go to the cafe [in Paris] that he inhabited to look at him. But that was the only literary man that I remember seeing in Europe in those days.'*

By the end of 1925 he had returned to the United States and learned within a few months that *Soldier's Pay*, in spite of being fairly well reviewed by the critics, was not selling well. He finished his second novel, *Mosquitoes*, and then returned to Oxford where he made his permanent home, taking various jobs as carpenter, painter, paper-hanger, and coal-heaver in an Oxford power plant. *Mosquitoes* was published in 1927 and also sold poorly. Two more of his novels, *Sartoris* and *The Sound and the Fury*, were published in 1929, the year that Faulkner married Estelle Oldham, whom he had known as a child. He still, however, made very little money out of writing, even when his fifth novel, *As I Lay Dying*, was published in 1930. It was with his sixth novel, *Sanctuary*, published in 1931 and reprinted a year later, that Faulkner achieved financial success. Money began to flow in, and one of his first purchases was a fine old mansion in Oxford. It required many repairs, and to help to pay for this he began to undertake work in which he was frequently to engage himself afterwards, as a script-writer in Hollywood. Faulkner's first child died, but in 1933 a daughter, Jill, was born, who became very close to her father.

Until after 1950 Faulkner avoided publicity, living a relatively quiet life in Oxford with his dogs and horses, and from time to time going on hunting trips. Although he liked to refer to himself as a farmer, he wrote steadily for the rest of his life. In 1946 Malcolm Cowley edited a selection of Faulkner's fiction in one volume called *The Portable Faulkner*, and since then the novelist's reputation has soared, both in America and internationally. In 1950 he was awarded the Nobel Prize for Literature, and he became something of a spokesman for the South after the decision of the United States Supreme Court requiring the integration of black and white pupils and students in Southern schools and universities.

*Faulkner in the University, Class Conferences at the University of Virginia, 1957–8, edited by Joseph L. Blotner and F.L. Gwynn, University of Virginia Press, Charlottesville, 1959, p.58.

William Faulkner died of a heart attack on 6 July 1962, and was buried in Oxford cemetery, in the town where he had lived for most of his life.

Faulkner and the South

The setting for most of Faulkner's short stories, and all but two of his eighteen novels, was the American South, and especially the state of Mississippi. Moreover, many of those stories and fifteen of the novels concern themselves with people who live in a small region of Northern Mississippi to which Faulkner gave the fictional title of Yoknapatawpha County. He drew a detailed map of this imaginary area, and referred to himself as its 'sole proprietor'. Faulkner wrote mainly about the histories, followed through several generations, of five white families and their black slaves or servants. *The Sound and the Fury* tells the story of the decline and fall into social and moral decay of one of these leading families, the Compsons.

By reading all of Faulkner's fiction, and particularly the short stories, it is possible to piece together the fictional sweep of his history of Yoknapatawpha County. The first stage begins with the white man's exploitation of the native Indians, bullying and cheating them out of their commonly held hunting grounds. Next comes the rape of the land itself, the uncaring destruction of timber and wild life for private gain, and not for need. Following that is the forced introduction of black people to serve in the establishment of a slave economy, and later the building of patterns of social behaviour to keep them in their inferior position after the abolition of slavery. The fourth stage comes after the American Civil War (1861–5), when the Northern States of America defeated the Confederation of Southern States. The Northern invaders exploit both blacks and defeated whites in the South. Those invaders are joined by Southern whites who are as grasping as the Northerners and who adopt their brutal principles. In the final stage of this history, a new breed of poor whites, whom Faulkner depicts through the Snopes clan in his fiction, moves in and completes the destruction of Southern aristocratic honour, now reduced by mismanagement and bankruptcy.

Even such a brief summary shows how closely Faulkner's fiction is involved with the history of the South's decay. Two of Faulkner's major themes are the white man's guilt about slavery, and the rape of the land; but what has come to be called Faulkner's 'legend of the South' is more complicated. He also felt that the destruction of the old South, by the Civil War and by the decades of 'reconstruction' which followed, released forces of corruption and disorder that had always been present in the South. These forces led to the decay of the old appearance of dignity and honour, and to the onset of a new, grasping commercialism. After the war, further changes came about as industry moved into the South, and political power gradually moved away from the old slaveholders and their social equals to the countless thousands of small tenant farmers who were known as 'rednecks'.

The story of the Compson family in *The Sound and the Fury* shows how they experience many of these social changes. They are forced to sell the last of their land so that Quentin can waste a year at Harvard University. In Mr Compson's high-sounding language we see values which no longer have any sense of purpose or direction. His wife Caroline worries uselessly about her genteel past which she has out-lived and can no longer afford. Their son Quentin owes his exaggerated sense of his sister Candace's duties and responsibilities to an equally out-of-date idea of Compson honour and of female purity. In another of Faulkner's novels, *Absalom, Absalom!*, Mr Compson remembers that 'years ago we in the South made our women into ladies. Then the war came and made the ladies into ghosts.' And when Faulkner was asked what was the trouble with the Compsons he replied: 'They are still living in the attitudes of 1859 or '60.'* But another of the Compson sons, Jason, lives according to the self-interested, commercial mentality which replaces earlier more decent values. Jason's attempt to survive his family's decay shows him to be worse than any of the Snopes who appear in other novels. As Faulkner himself once said: 'there are too many Jasons in the South who can be successful, just as there are too many Quentins in the South who are too sensitive to face its reality.'† The noblest character in *The Sound and the Fury*, the servant Dilsey, continues the story of black oppression and suffers from the Compsons' selfishness and pride. The final image of the castrated idiot Benjy holding a broken narcissus shocks us into recognising how a once proud family has been brought down by vanity to the tragic condition of self-regarding impotence.

Faulkner looked at this whole varied history of the South with mixed feelings of intimate affection, contempt, and controlled detach-ment. As a child he had listened eagerly to stories and legends about the men who had fought in the Civil War, and these memories of a chivalric and romantic past clashed with the circumstances of changed and changing fortunes which he saw around him. Faulkner felt those changes sharply since his own family had played a significant part in the story of the South. Many of the exciting tales he had listened to as a boy concerned the violent and colourful history of his own great-grandfather, Colonel William C. Falkner (1825–89), after whom he was named.

Faulkner in the University, p.18.
†*Faulkner in the University*, p.17.

In Oxford, Mississippi, Faulkner lived with the physical evidence of an older world, and he gradually found that his own knowledge and memory contained enough material for his novels. He dedicated *Go Down, Moses*, for example, to Caroline Barr, 'who was born in slavery and who gave to my family a fidelity without stint or calculation of recompense and to my childhood an immeasurable devotion and love'. It seems clear that in some way Caroline Barr helped Faulkner to forge his wonderful portrait of Dilsey in *The Sound and the Fury*. Faulkner's own comment about the ways in which he used his knowledge and experience of the South is appropriate. 'Beginning with *Sartoris* I discovered that my own little patch of native soil was worth writing about and that I would never live long enough to exhaust it . . . It opened up a gold mine of other people, so I created a cosmos of my own.'*

Literary influences

In 1921 the literary magazine *The Double Dealer* was established in New Orleans, and in 1922 the influential poetry magazine *The Fugitive* was founded in Nashville, Tennessee. Around these two publications grew a movement later called the Southern Renaissance, and this development, and some of the ideas associated with it, affected Faulkner to some extent, since he was himself involved. But whenever Faulkner was asked about the influences upon his own work he usually mentioned European writers rather than contemporary Americans, although he did think that Mark Twain was 'the first truly American writer', and that 'we all descended from him'.† Faulkner also tells us that he frequently read and studied the Bible during his childhood, and he also claimed to have re-read every year the classic novel by Miguel de Cervantes (1547–1616), *Don Quixote* (1605). He considered the French novelist Honoré de Balzac (1799–1850) to be the greatest of prose writers, and he acknowledged Joseph Conrad (1857–1924) to be a particular master.

It is often said that Faulkner was also considerably influenced by two works published in 1922, *The Waste Land* by T.S. Eliot (1888–1965), and *Ulysses* by James Joyce (1882–1941). *The Waste Land* may partly have suggested Faulkner's method, in *The Sound and the Fury*, of placing together several different sorts of narrative to give a broader view of a history. Similar techniques were also used by Joyce in *Ulysses*, a novel which presents the events of one day in a variety of styles and points of view not obviously connected by a story. Faulkner may also have learned from Joyce the 'stream-of-consciousness' (or

William Faulkner: Three Decades of Criticism, edited by Frederick J. Hoffman and Olga W. Vickery, Michigan State College Press, East Lansing, 1960, p.82.
†*Faulkner at Nagano*, edited by Robert A. Jelliffe, Kenkyusha, Tokyo, 1956, p.88.

'interior monologue') technique. Joyce was one of the first novelists to use this method of rendering directly, and as exactly as possible, the continuous flow of associated thoughts, feelings, words, memories, ideas and reflections as they pass through a character's mind. Because these thoughts and impressions are presented without comment or explanation from the author, they seem to be the contents of the character's mind itself. Faulkner uses this sort of technique in the first two sections of *The Sound and the Fury*, and he uses a similar technique in the third.

Both Joyce and Faulkner may have been encouraged in their use of stream of consciousness by the original work in psychoanalysis of Sigmund Freud (1856–1939). Freud's investigation of dreams and disturbed or unconscious mental states created a good deal of interest in the nature of the human mind and its workings. Faulkner's record of the operation of the mind of an idiot, Benjy, in the first section of *The Sound and the Fury* suggests this sort of interest.

The first two sections of *The Sound and the Fury* (April Seventh, 1928, and June Second, 1910) seem to concern the events of only two days. But Faulkner's stream-of-consciousness method in these sections really presents a broad history of the Compson family through Benjy's and Quentin's habit of continually associating the memories of past events with their present experience. This way of breaking up the normal progress of time and history, and Quentin's destruction of his watch, may perhaps suggest another influence on Faulkner – the French philosopher Henri Bergson (1859–1941). Bergson favoured the idea of time as open and freely flowing rather than counted in an exact, restricting way by clocks. Faulkner once remarked: 'I agree pretty much with Bergson's theory of the fluidity of time. There is only the present moment in which I include both the past and the future.'*

Both Bergson's ideas and those of Freud influenced much of the literature written in the 1920s. Critics sometimes use the term 'Modernism' to describe some of the art of this period. The term is applied to poetry, painting, fiction, music, and other art forms, and tries to group together various new and original kinds of presentation which were employed in the arts at this time. Novelists such as James Joyce and Virginia Woolf (1882–1941) are often called 'Modernist' because of their use of original techniques (like the stream of consciousness) and their rejection of the traditional ways of telling a story. Since William Faulkner, especially in *The Sound and the Fury*, often used similar new and unusual forms of presentation, he, also, has been considered as a 'Modernist'.

*Joseph Blotner, *Faulkner: a Biography,* 2 vols., Chatto and Windus, London, 1974, p.1441.

A note on the text

After being rejected by Harcourt, Brace and Company *The Sound and the Fury* was first published by Jonathan Cape and Harrison Smith, New York, in 1929. An English edition soon followed, published by Chatto and Windus, London, in 1931. This edition contained a short introduction by the novelist Richard Hughes (1900–76), excusing some of the apparent difficulties of the novel. Several other editions have been published since.

When Malcolm Cowley edited *The Portable Faulkner* in 1946, Faulkner provided an 'Appendix' which attempts to make *The Sound and the Fury* clearer by setting out character sketches and notes on several members of the Compson household. This interesting appendix appears in several of the later editions of *The Sound and the Fury*. For example, it is included as a foreword to *The Sound and the Fury and As I Lay Dying*, published by Random House, New York, in 1946. If this appendix is included, it is better placed at the end of the novel, and most more recent editions do this.

A standard modern edition was published by Chatto and Windus, London, in 1966, as part of *The Collected Works of William Faulkner*. This volume, and the paperback edition published by Penguin Books, Harmondsworth, in 1946, omit the appendix but include Richard Hughes's introduction. Other American paperback editions are also available.

Part 2

Summaries
of THE SOUND AND THE FURY

Note: Before reading the following summaries, it would be useful to look at the first section of Part 4 of these notes.

A difficulty with *The Sound and the Fury* is that Quentin, son of Mr and Mrs Compson and brother of Benjy, Caddy and Jason, has the same name as Caddy's illegitimate daughter, Quentin. To avoid the confusion which arises from this, Caddy's daughter will be referred to as 'Miss Quentin' throughout the following summaries and the rest of these notes.

A general summary

Although *The Sound and the Fury* seems to present the events of only four days, the story of the Compson family can be put together from the memories of the characters presented in the first three sections of the novel. The following is such a reconstruction of the events in the Compson family from 1898 to 1928.

Jason Compson, a lawyer and the descendant of 'governors and generals', marries Caroline Bascomb, a proud, selfish and genteel woman. They have four children: Quentin (born 1890), Caddy (born 1892), Jason (born 1894) and Maury (born 1895). One day in 1898 the children are playing in the stream when they are called back to the house for supper. Afterwards they come out again into the garden and Caddy, climbing a tree, tries to look through a window to find out what is happening in the house. The children are sure something is wrong, but are put to bed without being told that their grandmother, Damuddy, has died.

When Maury is five, Mrs Compson at last realises that he is growing up an idiot, and decides to change his name to avoid the connection with her brother, Uncle Maury, who also lives in the Compson household. So in 1900, Maury is renamed Benjamin (often shortened to Benjy). Mrs Compson still does not know how to treat him, and often thinks the strain of her 'burdens' makes her ill.

Even at an early age, Caddy and Quentin are very fond of one another. Caddy has to be allowed to go to school the year after Quentin, in order to remain near him, and Quentin fights anyone who offends or insults her.

Uncle Maury has an affair with Mrs Patterson, a woman who lives nearby, and, one cold day at Christmas time, he uses Caddy and Benjy as messengers to her. Later, he sends Benjy by himself, but this time Mr Patterson takes the letter from Benjy, discovers the affair, and fights Uncle Maury, hurting him. Uncle Maury recovers in bed, to the amusement of Mr Compson.

Mrs Compson thinks mostly of herself and her health, which she considers very poor, leaving the servant, Dilsey, largely in charge of the family. Because Mrs Compson seems unable to look after Benjy, Caddy often takes care of him. Benjy, like Quentin, is completely attached to his sister. As Caddy grows up, both Benjy and Quentin fear losing her love as she begins to be attracted by other men. Caddy first uses perfume in 1906, when she is fourteen, and Benjy is very upset until she washes it off. On one occasion in 1907, Mrs Compson discovers that Caddy has kissed a boy, and takes this as such a shock to her refined nature that she dresses in black, as if in mourning.

Benjy is also growing up. In 1908, when he is thirteen, it is decided that he must no longer share a bed with Caddy, although she still remains with him and comforts him until he falls asleep in his own bed. One moonlit evening about this time he slips out into the garden and finds Caddy sitting in the swing embracing a young man. Benjy howls until Caddy runs back into the house with him, washes out her mouth, and promises it will never happen again. But in 1909 she falls passionately in love with a stranger, Dalton Ames, and loses her virginity. Benjy senses what has happened and is deeply upset.

Caddy's loss of virginity has an even greater effect on Quentin. When they were children, Quentin's strange games with a girl called Natalie seemed to involve his sexual feeling for his sister, especially when he later rubbed mud all over her. He also resented Caddy's kissing the boy. His involvement with his sister remains intense throughout his life. When it is discovered that she has had sexual contact with Dalton Ames, Caddy runs from the house to the stream to wash herself. Quentin follows and urges her to commit suicide along with him. Caddy refuses to help him to kill her. Quentin later meets Dalton Ames, and in the name of the family honour, tells him with various threats that he must leave town. But Dalton is too strong for him, and Quentin faints instead of fighting. As he recovers, Caddy explains to him how much she loves Dalton.

Shortly afterwards, Quentin goes away for a year at Harvard University. His education there is paid for by the sale of the pasture next to the Compson garden where Benjy used to play. The money also helps to pay for Mr Compson's heavy drinking. The pasture is made into a golf course.

After Dalton Ames, Caddy continues to have lovers until she becomes pregnant and has to find a husband. She marries Herbert

Head, a bank manager, who flatters Mrs Compson, buys Caddy a car, and offers Jason a job in his bank. He also tries to make friends with Quentin, who returned home from Harvard at Christmas time and now comes back again for the wedding. But Quentin has learned some unpleasant facts about Head's behaviour at Harvard, and confronts him with them. He also tries to tell Caddy, and prevent her from marrying him, but she becomes angry with him.

On the wedding day, in 1910, the servant T.P. finds champagne in the cellar. He is looking after Benjy, and both get quickly drunk. Benjy disrupts the reception by bellowing outside. Caddy runs out to comfort him, while Quentin deals with T.P.

Disturbed by the 'loss' of his sister, and increasingly obsessed with her sexuality, with time, and with his own ideas of guilt, incest and honour, Quentin returns unhappily to Harvard. We learn in detail about June Second, 1910, the last day of his life there: how he breaks his watch; arranges his affairs; wanders around; meets a little Italian girl; fights her brother, and later a fellow student; continually remembers Caddy and the past; and eventually drowns himself.

Now that she has married and has moved away, Benjy sadly misses Caddy. He likes to go and look for her at the gate, where she used to return home from school each day. One day he frightens some schoolgirls there. On another occasion, finding the gate has been left open, he goes out and attacks a girl. To prevent any further episodes such as this, Benjy has to be castrated (1910).

Caddy's marriage to Herbert Head does not last long, perhaps because he discovers that he is not the father of her child, whom she names Quentin in memory of her brother. Mr Compson travels north to fetch the child and bring it back to the Compson household. Mrs Compson is so shocked by her daughter's actions that she forbids any further mention of Caddy's name. Jason always bitterly regrets the loss of his chance to work in Herbert Head's bank.

Mr Compson has continued drinking increasingly heavily, against the advice of his doctors. While the household is still recovering from the suicide of Quentin, Mr Compson dies (1912). Mrs Compson and Uncle Maury return by carriage from the burial, leaving Jason behind in the graveyard. There he meets Caddy, who has returned in secret for the funeral. For a price, Jason agrees to let her see Miss Quentin, but cheats her, allowing her only a glimpse of the child. Jason refuses to let Caddy see her again, and forces her to agree to send money to Mrs Compson for Miss Quentin's welfare. With his mother's help, Jason gets a job in a hardware store. He continues to cheat Caddy, his mother and Miss Quentin, by a clever and criminal scheme of cashing Caddy's cheques himself.

After Mr Compson's death, Benjy and Mrs Compson start regular visits by carriage to the graveyard. Jason refuses to come with them. Now that his father is dead, and Uncle Maury only continues to drink and beg money from Mrs Compson, Jason is head of the Compson household. Miss Quentin grows up unhappily in the atmosphere of lovelessness and cruelty which his unpleasant character creates. Like Caddy, she becomes involved with many young men. She attends school irregularly, cannot be controlled by Mrs Compson, and always quarrels bitterly and violently with Jason. Such is the situation on the morning of April Sixth, 1928.

Partly because Mrs Compson's pride and selfishness make her such an incompetent mother, the Compson children are cared for by a family of Negro servants. Dilsey and her husband Roskus have two sons, Versh and T.P., and a daughter, Frony, who has a son, Luster. Roskus suffers very badly from rheumatism, and he dies some time after Mr Compson. Versh goes off to Memphis. In 1928, Luster has grown up to the job of looking after Benjy, while Dilsey alone remains to look after Miss Quentin and the rest of the Compson household.

On April Sixth we follow in detail the events of Jason's day. He quarrels as usual with Miss Quentin; argues with his boss; loses money on the stock market; works at his scheme for cheating Caddy; sees Miss Quentin playing truant (she is walking around the town with a man from the travelling show); pursues her unsuccessfully; and returns home to behave unpleasantly at dinner.

April Seventh is Benjy's birthday, and we follow him as he wanders around, looked after by Luster, continually recalling Caddy and the past.

On April Eighth 1928, Easter Sunday, we see Dilsey looking after the Compson household, and taking Benjy, Frony and Luster to the Negro church. Jason finds that Miss Quentin has robbed him of all his money (mostly stolen from her), climbed down the tree outside her window, and run away with the man from the travelling show. He furiously but unsuccessfully pursues them to the town of Mottson. Returning to Jefferson, he finds Benjy bellowing with shocked surprise as Luster drives him on an unfamiliar route to the cemetery. Jason turns them round and restores order to Benjy's idiot mind.

Detailed summaries

April Seventh, 1928

Here, Benjy's thoughts on April Seventh, 1928, are recorded. This record is not only of Benjy's responses to his experience on that day, but also of his repeated memories of several incidents from his earlier life. As Benjy is an idiot, his thoughts do not follow one another logically or directly. Several earlier experiences are connected by him both with each other and with what is happening on April Seventh, 1928. The result is a confusing mixture of previous incidents and present experience. To make the record of Benjy's thoughts clearer, the following summaries separate his present experience and the several episodes from the past which he remembers.

Damuddy's death (1898)

(1) The Compson children are playing in the stream, looked after by Versh. Caddy is wet and asks Versh to take her dress off. Quentin slaps her: she falls in the stream, then splashes water on Quentin, Versh and Benjy. Jason is playing by himself. Caddy soothes Benjy. (2) Roskus comes to tell them that it is time for supper. The children argue about telling their parents that they have got wet, then (3) begin to return to their brightly lit home. (4) Quentin remains behind; Versh carries Benjy. At the back door they meet Mr Compson, who tells them to be quiet and eat in the kitchen. He says that there are guests in the house, and allows Caddy to be in charge of the children. While they are eating, they hear their mother crying. Dilsey wants the children to go quietly to bed, but Caddy leads them back outside. (5) With Versh, they go down to the servants' house, leaving Quentin behind. Frony and T.P. are playing with a bottle of fireflies there. (6) They begin to talk about funerals. (7) Frony reveals that Damuddy is dead. Caddy remembers the horse Nancy, who had to be shot when she fell into a ditch. (8) Caddy still believes there is a party in their house, and leads everyone back to look. (9) On the way, they see a snake. (10) Versh carries Benjy. (11) Caddy climbs a tree to get a better view into the house through the windows. Dilsey discovers them, sends T.P. and Frony back to their house, and takes the others back into the kitchen, telling Versh to look for Quentin. (12) She refuses Caddy's offer to carry Benjy upstairs. They pass Mr Compson, who looks grim. (13) He says that Mrs Compson is sick, and tells the children to be quiet. (14) Dilsey takes the children to a spare room, and undresses Benjy. (15) Versh brings in Quentin, who is crying. (16) Dilsey discovers Caddy's wet, muddy clothes, and leaves the children to sleep. Their father comes to say goodnight to them. Benjy, sleeping in the same bed as Caddy, feels the dark and sees the light coming in the morning.

Benjy is renamed (1900)

(1) One rainy day, Caddy and Mrs Compson are in the library with Benjy, who is looking at the fire. Caddy tries to teach him that his name has been changed from Maury to Benjy. He howls when Caddy tries to carry him over to his mother, who wants him to be led instead. She criticises Caddy for trying to carry him; for shortening Benjamin to

Benjy; and for generally spoiling him. Left with his mother, Benjy cries, until Caddy reassures him, showing him his cushion. Mrs Compson, upset by his behaviour, lies back in her chair and cries too. (2) Caddy goes to the kitchen, taking Benjy with her, to fetch Dilsey, who scolds her for upsetting her mother. Caddy explains how this happened. Dilsey goes to look after Mrs Compson, and Caddy herself begins to cry, laying her head in Benjy's lap. (3) Dilsey returns, learns disapprovingly of Benjy's change of name, and refers to her own religious belief that she will be called Dilsey for ever. Later (4) Mr Compson comes into the library. He talks to Benjy, and restrains Caddy, who is fighting Jason because he cut up Benjy's paper dolls. (5) Caddy reassures Benjy, showing him the fire, the mirror and the cushion. (6) Quentin comes in, and Caddy notices that he has been in a fight. (7) Mr Compson returns from punishing Jason, who remains outside, crying, and asks about the fight. (8) Quentin explains that he fought another boy who threatened to put a frog in Caddy's desk at school. Mr Compson calls Jason in and comforts him. (9) Dilsey calls the family to dinner. Benjy remains in the library, and Versh comes to look after him. He smells of the rain which falls heavily outside, and tells Benjy a strange story about the change of his name. Then he begins to dry his legs in front of the fire, pushing Benjy aside. Caddy wants to feed Benjy, and takes him away to the kitchen, where (11) Roskus is drying off in front of the stove. (12) Benjy eats hungrily, while (13) Dilsey and Roskus talk about the rain, and about Mrs Compson. (14) Versh carries Benjy up to Mrs Compson's room. Lying in bed, she says goodnight to Benjy and Caddy, but complains that it is too early for Benjy to go to bed. Mr Compson takes the children down to the library again, (15) asking them to be quiet as Quentin is studying. He tells Jason to stop chewing paper, and holds Caddy and Benjy on his knee in the firelight.

Christmas-time (23 December)
(1) One cold day just before Christmas (23 December), Benjy wants to go out to meet Caddy returning from school. Mrs Compson worries about the cold, and complains about her problems, but Uncle Maury persuades her to let Versh dress Benjy and take him out. Caddy meets him, and warms his hands, which he has put on the cold gate. (2) Together they run back to the house, where Uncle Maury passes a message to Caddy, and persuades Mrs Compson, who is still complaining about her situation, to let Caddy and Benjy go back outside. Benjy is dressed for outdoors again. Caddy embraces him, and they depart furtively across the garden, taking Uncle Maury's message to Mrs Patterson, who lives nearby. (3) Benjy's clothes get caught on the fence, and Caddy frees him, telling him (4) to keep his hands warm in

his pockets. They pass the pig-pen, go round the barn, and cross the frozen stream near where a pig is being slaughtered. Caddy thinks the letter is a sort of Christmas present. She climbs over a fence and delivers it to Mrs Patterson.

Uncle Maury and Mrs Patterson
(1) On another occasion, Uncle Maury sends Benjy to Mrs Patterson by himself. She sees Benjy and runs to get the letter, but her dress catches in the fence and her husband, who is working in the garden, reaches it first. Benjy runs away. Later, Mr Patterson fights Uncle Maury, blackening his eye and hurting his mouth. (2) He recovers in bed, while Mr Compson makes fun of him and his affair with Mrs Patterson.

Caddy uses perfume (1906)
Caddy cannot discover what is disturbing Benjy, who is very upset. His mother, lying sick in bed, hears him moaning, calls them into the room, and accuses Caddy of teasing Benjy. For a while he is quietened by looking at his mother's jewellery box, but then he follows Caddy, moaning again. Mrs Compson asks her husband to take him downstairs, but Benjy ignores T.P.'s calls and waits outside the bathroom for Caddy, who is washing. When she reappears, he is quiet. When Caddy takes him to her room and lets him smell the perfume that she has been wearing, she realises what had upset him. Benjy loves Caddy to 'smell like trees', and was disturbed by the change in her scent. She takes Benjy downstairs and makes him give her perfume to Dilsey as a present.

Caddy in the swing
(1) One moonlit evening, Benjy is being looked after by T.P., but wanders away from him and goes out into the garden, passing the dog Dan. (2) He sees Caddy and a man, Charlie, embracing in the garden swing. He begins to cry. (3) Caddy comes to comfort him, but is followed by Charlie. He tells her to send Benjy away, and tries to hold her and pull her away from him. Benjy cries really loudly. Caddy frees herself from Charlie and says she will take Benjy inside and then return, but she runs back into the house with Benjy, washes her mouth out, and, crying with him, promises she will not go out to meet young men any more.

Benjy has to sleep alone (1908)
Dilsey tells Benjy (who is thirteen) that he is too grown up to sleep with Caddy any longer, and must go to bed by himself in Uncle Maury's room. But Dilsey discovers that Benjy will not stop crying or go to sleep until Caddy comes to him. Without undressing, Caddy stays with Benjy until he falls asleep.

Caddy's loss of virginity (1909)

Caddy has broken her promise to Benjy, and been with a man. (1) She is called into the room by her parents. She cannot look at Benjy and moves away from him when he comes towards her, crying. (2) She retreats upstairs, crying herself. Benjy follows her, pulls her towards the bathroom, and tries to push her in as she hides her face from him with her arm.

Caddy's wedding (1910)

(1) As the guests return to the house to celebrate Caddy's wedding, Dilsey (who is busy with the preparations) tells T.P. to take Benjy outside. T.P. thinks there is soda water, which he later (2) calls 'sassprilluh', in the cellar. In fact it is champagne, and when T.P. and Benjy drink a bottle, both quickly become drunk. (3) T.P. fetches a box so that they can look through the window at the party. (4) Benjy climbs on the box and sees Caddy in her wedding dress, and begins to howl for her. T.P. takes him back to the cellar to drink more. They are now very drunk; they fall over, then rush out into the garden again. Benjy, howling, tries to climb on to the box, but falls, hurts himself, and begins to bellow. Quentin and Caddy come out of the house. Caddy tries to console Benjy, who still cries because she no longer 'smells like trees'. Quentin kicks and strikes T.P. and (5) takes him and Benjy to the barn. He throws T.P. repeatedly against the wall, but he remains as drunk as ever. Benjy's impressions are completely disordered by the effects of the champagne. Quentin leaves to get help. Versh appears and asks where the drink came from. Quentin returns with a hot drink to make Benjy sick. With Versh's help, he lays Benjy in a crib.

Benjy in the garden (1910)

(1) Even after Caddy is married and has left home, Benjy still waits for her at the garden gate, crying. When he is inside, he still wants to go back out to the gate. One day, when T.P. and Mrs Compson are discussing this, (2) he slips out and, on his side of the fence, follows some schoolgirls who are walking by. He tries to communicate with them, but only frightens them. T.P. comes out to find him, and scolds him. (3) On another occasion, Benjy slips out and finds the gate is open. Schoolgirls walk by, confident that he cannot get out. But Benjy does get out, catches one of them, and frightens her very badly. Later (4) Jason and Mr Compson ask how he could have escaped. Jason criticises the family and states his opinion that Benjy must now be sent to the state asylum in the town of Jackson. But, instead, Benjy is castrated. His memories of attacking the girl merge into his memories of this operation.

Quentin's death (1910)

(1) The Compsons have learned of Quentin's death at Harvard.

Dilsey, crying in the kitchen, tells T.P. to keep Benjy out of the house. They play in the stream, return to the house, then go to the barn, where Roskus, troubled by rheumatism, milks a cow with one hand. He complains of the bad luck that surrounds the Compson household. (2) That night, Benjy sleeps in the servants' house, in T.P.'s bed. Before going to sleep, he listens to the conversation in the firelight. Roskus talks of death, bad luck, and the misfortunes of the Compsons. T.P. has seen signs of death: a screech-owl and a howling dog. Dilsey is more cheerful, pointing out to Roskus his personal good fortune and concluding that in any case all men will die one day.

Mr Compson's death (1912)
(1) Benjy is upset and lies howling in his bed. He can hear his mother crying. T.P. gets him out of bed, dresses him, and starts to take him to the servants' house. Benjy thinks his father is sick, and sees a stranger in his room. Dilsey tries to quieten him, and then sends him downstairs with T.P. Outside, they pass the dog, Dan, who is howling. Benjy moans very loudly. T.P. takes him on past the pig-pen and across the stream, where Benjy stumbles and gets partly wet. They finally stop near the ditch where the horse Nancy was killed. Here Benjy's bellowing can disturb no one. (2) On the next evening, Dilsey tells T.P. to take Benjy and Miss Quentin down to the servants' house. Luster, Benjy, and Miss Quentin play there, and Frony scolds Benjy for taking the others' toys. She takes them all to the barn, where T.P. is milking, watched by Roskus. Frony asks them to look after Benjy. T.P. takes him back to the servants' house, where Roskus complains again about the Compson family and their bad luck, and of the fact that Caddy's name is never mentioned now, even to her own daughter. Despite Frony's protests, Dilsey puts Benjy to bed with Luster, telling him to be careful of the sleeping child. (3) At Mr Compson's funeral, T.P. restrains Benjy while the carriages leave for the cemetery. (4) Then he takes Miss Quentin and Benjy to watch the hearse going past, with Mr Compson's coffin inside.

Trip to the cemetery (1913)
One day Mrs Compson wants to visit the graves of her husband and her son. Dilsey puts Benjy in the carriage to go with her. Roskus suffers badly from rheumatism, so T.P. must drive, despite Mrs Compson's protests. Dilsey reassures her, takes one of her flowers to quieten Benjy, and warns T.P. to be careful. But Mrs Compson is still alarmed by his driving, and tells him to turn around and go back. His efforts to do so frighten her still more, and so they continue. They pass the centre of town, and meet Jason, who sourly refuses to come with them. They go on to the cemetery.

Roskus's death

Dilsey and her family moan and weep over the death of her husband Roskus. The dog, Blue, howls too. Frony tells Luster she needs to be left in peace to cook, but Luster refuses to take anyone away to the barn, which he says is haunted by Roskus.

The present (April Seventh, 1928)

(1) It is Benjy's thirty-third birthday. Looked after by Luster, he watches some golfers from the Compson garden. Their use of the word 'caddie' upsets him, reminding him of his sister. Luster tries to quieten his moaning, and leads him along the garden fence to the stream. Crawling through the fence, Benjy's clothes catch on a nail. (2) He moans because the golfers have gone. Luster gives him a flower to quieten him (3) but Benjy moans again when he remembers Caddy. They pass the carriage house and (4) go through the broken-down barn. Luster warns Benjy to stay away from the golf course. (5) They go down to the stream, where other Negroes are doing their washing. Benjy still wants to return to the golf course, but Luster is looking for a coin (a quarter) that he has lost. He needs it in order to go to a travelling show that is in town that night, which he discusses with the other Negroes. A golf ball comes down from the golf course, and Luster keeps it from the caddies who come to look for it. Mention of 'caddie' makes Benjy moan, and Luster encourages him to play in the stream. (6) Benjy's memories of Caddy upset him again, and the other Negroes complain. (7) Luster takes him away to look for the quarter elsewhere, and (8) to take his golf ball home. Benjy is attracted by the ball. (9) Luster is still worried about his quarter. (10) Benjy strays towards the golf course again, and Luster, having an idea, goes to fetch his ball, (11) warning Benjy to stay away from Miss Quentin and a showman with a red tie who are sitting in the garden swing. (12) But Benjy wanders over to them, and they hurriedly separate from an embrace. Miss Quentin is furious and accuses Luster of letting Benjy follow her around. (13) Luster excuses himself. The showman does a match-trick for Benjy, annoying Miss Quentin (who runs off) by encouraging him to try it too. The showman discusses Benjy with Luster, who tries to beg a quarter and then to sell his golf ball. Luster takes Benjy off towards the golf course, finding a bright object under a bush. The showman recognises it and asks Luster who had visited Miss Quentin the night before. Luster explains that she is visited by men every night she can climb down the tree outside her window to meet them. He continues to look for his quarter. Benjy is upset because he cannot see any golfers, and moves off to the garden gate. Luster calls him back, (14) telling him to be quiet, and (15) tries unsuccessfully to sell his golf ball to a golfer who simply takes it from him. Benjy is

upset once more when he hears the word 'caddie'. Luster tries to quieten him, and gives him a flower. Benjy puts it into a bottle, along with another flower, in the area called his 'graveyard'. Luster begins to tease him, taking away his flower and whispering 'Caddy' to him. Dilsey hears Benjy's loud bellows, angrily calls Luster, and accuses him of upsetting Benjy. Seated in front of the fire that burns in the kitchen stove, Benjy quietens down. (16) Dilsey continues to scold Luster. She gives Benjy his birthday cake, first lighting the candles. But when she leaves the room, Luster blows them out and (17) begins to eat most of the cake himself. He closes the stove door with a long piece of wire, and Benjy howls at the loss of his comforting view of the fire. Dilsey returns and scolds Luster. (18) When he closes the stove door a second time, Dilsey catches him, shouts at him and shakes him. Meanwhile, Benjy reaches for the fire and burns himself. Dilsey hits Luster and tends Benjy, whose screaming attracts his mother. She complains of being disturbed while she is ill, and begins to cry. Dilsey takes her away, then returns to quieten Benjy by giving him a familiar slipper. Luster takes him to the library and lights a fire for him, but he continues to cry. (19) Jason comes in and (20) demands that Luster keep Benjy quiet. (21) Supper is ready, and Dilsey looks for Miss Quentin. (22) Luster asks Jason for a quarter and is coldly refused. Miss Quentin comes into the library, and Jason angrily discusses her association with the showman. (23) Jason and Miss Quentin both complain about Benjy, whose memories of Caddy have made him moan again. (24) Miss Quentin especially dislikes eating with him at table. (25) She says she will run away. (26) Jason angers her even more, and, although restrained by Dilsey, she tries to throw a glass at him, before (27) running out of the room and back to the library. (28) Later, at nightfall, Benjy goes to a dark empty room, still clutching his slipper. Luster, who has got a quarter from Miss Quentin, finds him there and takes him to his bedroom. (29) Mrs Compson locks Miss Quentin in her bedroom and asks for a hot-water bottle. (30) Benjy undresses, crying. Luster quietens him. Together they watch Miss Quentin climb down the tree outside her bedroom window. Luster puts Benjy to bed and goes off to see the show.

Benjy's mind switches frequently between the episodes summarised above. These changes of episode are usually indicated in the novel by a change from normal to *italic* type. To help to make clear which of the episodes each part of the first section of *The Sound and the Fury* is about, there is a list below of the first words of each part in normal or *italic* type, followed by a note of the episodes each of these parts concerns. The numbers in brackets refer to the numbers in the summaries above.

Through the fence — present (1)
Caddy uncaught me — Christmas-time (3)
It's too cold out there — Christmas-time (1)
What are you moaning about — present (2)
'What is it.' Caddy said — Christmas-time (2)
Can't you shut up that moaning — present (3)
Git in now, and set still — trip to the cemetery
Cry baby, Luster said — present (4)
Keep your hands in your pockets — Christmas-time (4)
Mr Patterson was chopping — Uncle Maury and Mrs Patterson (1)
They ain't nothing over yonder — present (5)
and Roskus came and said — Damuddy's death (2)
She was wet — Damuddy's death (1)
What is the matter with you — present (6)
Roskus came and said — Damuddy's death (2)
See you all at the show tonight — present (7)
If we go slow, it'll be dark — Damuddy's death (3)
The cows came jumping — Caddy's wedding (5)
'Go on.' T.P. said — Caddy's wedding (5)
At the top of the hill — Damuddy's death (4)
Come on here, Quentin — Damuddy's death (4)
There was a fire in it — Quentin's death (2)
Then I got up — Quentin's death (1)
Tain't no luck on this place — Quentin's death (2)
What you know about it — Quentin's death (2)
Take him and Quentin down to the house — Mr Compson's death (2)
We finished eating — Mr Compson's death (2)
You can't go yet — Mr Compson's death (3)
We looked around the corner — Mr Compson's death (4)
Come on, Luster said — present (8)
Frony and T.P. were playing — Damuddy's death (5)
They moaned at Dilsey's house — Roskus's death
'Oh.' Caddy said — Damuddy's death (6)
Dilsey moaned — Roskus's death
I like to know why not — Damuddy's death (7). Remembering
    Caddy's mention of the bones of the horse Nancy, Benjy's mind
    passes on to Mr Compson's death (1). This change of episode begins
    at 'The bones rounded out of the ditch', and it is not indicated by a
    change in type.
I had it when we was down here before — present (9)
Do you think buzzards — Damuddy's death (8)
When we looked around the corner — Caddy's wedding (1)
A snake crawled out — Damuddy's death (9)
You ain't got to start — Caddy's wedding (2)

We stopped under the tree — Damuddy's death (10)

They getting ready to start — Caddy's wedding (3)

We drank the sassprilluh — Caddy's wedding (3). Benjy's memory of
looking through the window at Caddy's wedding moves straight on
to memories of looking through the window at the time of Damuddy's
death (11). The change occurs at 'They haven't started because the
band hasn't come yet'. It is not indicated by a change of type.

I saw them — Caddy's wedding (4)

'Hush.' T.P. said — Caddy's wedding (4)

Benjy, Caddy said, Benjy — Caddy uses perfume

'What is it, Benjy.' she said — Caddy uses perfume

She smelled like trees — This is a repeated sensation of Benjy's,
continually associated with Caddy.

'Come on, now.' Dilsey said — Benjy has to sleep alone. From 'Uncle
Maury was sick', Benjy's mind goes back to Uncle Maury and
Mrs Patterson (2). From '"You a big boy." Dilsey said', he returns
to being told he must sleep alone. Neither of these changes is
indicated by a change in type.

We looked up into the tree — Damuddy's death (11)

Where you want to go now — present (10)

The kitchen was dark — Caddy in the swing (1)

Luster came back — present (11)

It was dark under the trees — Caddy in the swing (2)

Come away from there — present (11)

It was two now — Caddy in the swing (3)

I kept a-telling you to stay away — present (12)

'I couldn't stop him.' Luster said — present (13)

You can't do no good looking through — Benjy in the garden (1)

I could hear them talking — Benjy in the garden (2)

How did he get out — Benjy in the garden (4)

It was open when I touched it — Benjy in the garden (3)

Here, loony, Luster said — present (14)

They came to the flag — present (15)

What you want to get her started for — Benjy is renamed (2)

Ain't you shamed of yourself — present (16)

I could hear the clock — Benjy is renamed (3)

I ate some cake — present (17)

That's right, Dilsey said — Benjy is renamed (3)

The long wire came across my shoulder — present (18)

Your name is Benjy — Benjy is renamed (1)

Caddy said. 'Let me carry him up' — Damuddy's death (12)

Versh set me down — Benjy is renamed (14)

Come and tell mother goodnight — Benjy is renamed (14)

Mother's sick, Father said — Damuddy's death (13)

Father stood and watched — Damuddy's death (13)
We could hear the roof. I could see the fire — Benjy is renamed (1)
'Come on, now.' she said — Benjy is renamed (1)
Jason came in — present (19)
He just trying hisself — present (20)
You can look at the fire — Benjy is renamed (5)
Dilsey said, 'You come, Jason' — present (21)
We could hear the roof. Quentin smelled like rain — Benjy is renamed (6)
Quentin said, 'Didn't Dilsey' — present (22)
I could hear the roof — Benjy is renamed (7)
'Nobody.' Quentin said — Benjy is renamed (8)
Dilsey said, All right — Benjy is renamed (9)
We could hear Caddy walking fast — Caddy's loss of virginity (1)
Versh said, Your name Benjamin now — Benjy is renamed (10)
We were in the hall — Caddy's loss of virginity (2)
What are you doing to him — present (23)
Versh said, 'You move back some' — Benjy is renamed (10)
Has he got to keep that dirty old slipper — present (24)
Steam came off Roskus — Benjy is renamed (11)
Now, now, Dilsey said — present (25)
It got down below the mark — Benjy is renamed (12)
Yes he will, Quentin said — present (25)
Roskus said, 'It going to rain' — Benjy is renamed (13)
You've been running a long time — present (26)
Then I don't know what — Benjy is renamed (13)
Oh, I wouldn't be surprised — present (26)
She sulling again — Benjy is renamed (13)
Quentin pushed Dilsey away — present (26)
Mother's sick again — Benjy is renamed (13)
Goddam you, Quentin said — present (29)
Caddy gave me the cushion — Benjy is renamed (15)
She smelled like trees — present (28)
We didn't go to our room — Damuddy's death (14)
Quentin, Mother said — present (29)
Quentin and Versh came in — Damuddy's death (15)
I got undressed — present (30)
There were two beds — Damuddy's death (16)

NOTES AND GLOSSARY:
Much of *The Sound and the Fury* is written in the Negro dialect of the Southern States of America. In the glossary which follows, only particularly difficult or unusual words or phrases are explained.
caddie: a golfer's attendant, who carries his clubs

quarter:	an American coin, worth twenty-five cents (one hundred cents make one dollar)
the branch:	a small stream
niggers:	(*slang*) Negroes, black people
snagged:	caught by the clothing
toddy:	a hot, alcoholic drink; usually whisky, hot water and sugar
hickeynuts:	hickory nuts (these are like walnuts)
jouncing:	bouncing and swinging
ahun:	iron
jimson weed:	Jamestown weed; a large, coarse weed with an unpleasant smell
surrey:	a four-wheeled carriage
the baby:	Mrs Compson means Benjy
projecking:	disturbing, interfering with
Hum up, Get up:	calls to the horse to make it speed up

the tall white post where the soldier was: a statue of a Confederate soldier in the square at the centre of Jefferson (the town nearest the Compsons' house)

loony:	a lunatic

drawing on you for fifty: borrowing fifty dollars from you
Prince, Queenie, and Fancy: the Compsons' horses

chillen:	children

got it at the getting place: Luster does not reveal where he got his quarter

I ain't studying no quarter: it's none of my business

bellering:	bellowing, crying loudly
biggity:	big-headed, conceited
hollered:	shouted
hot dog, whooey:	expressions of joy or surprise
sassprilluh:	sarsaparilla, a fizzy soft drink
wear you out:	beat you severely

chunking into the shadows where the branch was: throwing stones into the stream

skizzard:	a term of abuse invented by the Compson children

let them mind me: let them take orders from me
the Lawd's own time: the Lord's own time; that is, soon enough; in due course
you got to tune up: stop crying and behave properly
chunking it into a blaze: building the fire up, throwing logs on to it
Dilsey was singing: probably she was moaning or crying
what trance you been in: what mistake have you been making?
the sign of it laying right there: Roskus suggests that Benjy is a sign of the Compson's bad luck

they been two now: two deaths, Damuddy's and Quentin's

a squinch owl: a screech-owl, whose cry was thought to be an omen of death

no luck in saying that name: Caddy's name, which is no longer mentioned in the Compson household

play pretty: a toy

them Memphis notions into Versh: Roskus's gloomy talk about death (two years previously) encouraged Versh to leave for the town of Memphis

I ain't got no wings: I can't go any faster

pointer: a dog used to scent game

conjure him: interfere with him or influence him badly

lightning bugs: fireflies

racket: noise

that bullfrog voice: a deep, loud voice like the cry of a bullfrog

buzzing grass: Benjy hears the noise of insects in the grass

knobknot: another term of abuse invented by the Compson children

prissy: pretending to be elegant or prim

Et ego in arcadia **I have forgotten the Latin for hay:** Mr Compson's Latin quotation means 'I too have been in paradise'. He wants to go on to explain that Uncle Maury's paradise was lying with Mrs Patterson in the hay in a barn, but has forgotten the Latin for this

a matched team: a pair of work horses

Satan: Caddy is misbehaving, and Dilsey uses the Devil's name to scold her

beau: (*French*) an admirer or lover; here, Miss Quentin's

loon: a stupid person, a lunatic

played hell: caused a lot of trouble

ricklick: recollect

mulehead: stupid person

Agnes Mabel Becky: a popular contraceptive at the time was sold in a shiny metal box with 'Agnes Mabel Becky' written on the lid. It is one of these (empty) boxes that Luster finds

a 'fraid cat: a coward

fore: a golfer's cry of warning to those who may get in the way of his shot

the bars: in the lunatic asylum at Jackson

don't you sass me: don't be cheeky

dogfennel: a weed with an unpleasant smell

truck: (*slang*) rubbish

trying yourself: deliberately behaving badly

Benjamin:	Caddy says that Benjy's new name comes from the Bible. The story of Benjamin is given in Genesis 42–5
the Book:	Dilsey has religious faith in a record-book in Heaven of good deeds on earth
years:	ears
soda:	used to ease the pain of burns
I'll be gone soon:	I'll soon be dead
liberry:	the library, a room in the Compson house

the dark tall place on the wall: a space on the wall where a mirror had once hung

minute:	Dilsey refers to the saying that children were 'no bigger than a minute'
tote:	carry
I'll slit his gizzle:	I'll slit his gizzard, or stomach; in other words, I'll kill him
two bits:	a quarter, twenty-five cents
bluegum:	a Negro who had blue gums instead of the normal pink ones was feared for the magic powers he was thought to possess
possum:	the opossum; a small, furry, wild animal

I'll skin your rinktum: I'll beat you on the bottom

sulling:	sulking, or pretending to be sick

let them horns toot: the signal for the start of the show which Luster wants to see

nighties:	pyjamas, night-wear
yessum:	yes, madam

Looking for them ain't going to do no good. They're gone: that is, Benjy's genitals have gone; he has been castrated

while my foots behaves: that is, while Luster hurries off to see the show

I bound you would: I'm sure you would

tattletale:	someone who 'tells tales' or reveals secrets

June Second, 1910

On this day Quentin Compson is to commit suicide by drowning. It is helpful to read this section as if it were written by a drowning man at the moment of his death, when, according to popular belief, the whole of his past life flashes through his mind. Quentin is very disturbed as he prepares to kill himself, and memories and recollections of his past life crowd into his brain in an apparently disorganised way. Nine events in time, including the present, form the substance of Quentin's narrative, and these are summarised below in chronological order.

(1) Damuddy's death (1898), and the changing of Benjy's name (1900)
In Quentin's mind, thoughts of the day that Damuddy died concentrate upon him fighting with his sister Caddy because she had taken off her dress at the stream. In her anger, Caddy threatens to run away, but when Benjy begins to cry she reassures him. Quentin's memories of this day mix with his memories of Dilsey's resentment at Benjy's name being changed from Maury. Throughout his narrative Quentin refers to Benjy's ability to 'smell' Damuddy's death.

(2) The childhood scene with Natalie
Quentin remembers Caddy and Natalie as children playing in the barn. When Caddy runs away, Quentin asks Natalie where Caddy had hurt her, and offers to carry Natalie. When he touches her, Quentin becomes excited and they then play a game in which they dance sitting down. Caddy, who watches this from the barn door, leaves, and Quentin runs after her. He then jumps into the muddy ditch where the hogs wallow. Quentin catches up with Caddy, mocking her and rubbing his mud on her dress. Caddy slaps him and Quentin pushes her to the ground, and smears her with mud. After she scratches him they both lie down exhausted. Quentin asks Caddy if she cares now. They go to the stream and sit in it to clean themselves, watching the mud float to the surface of the water.

(3) Caddy kisses a boy
Quentin remembers Caddy mocking him by telling him that she had forced a boy to kiss her. Again Quentin pushes her to the ground. He rubs her head in the grass and tells her to surrender by saying 'calf-rope'. Caddy's reply is 'I didn't kiss a dirty girl like Natalie anyway'. When she learns that Caddy has kissed a boy, Mrs Compson tries to show her horror by dressing in black.

(4) Caddy's loss of virginity (1909)
Several events are mixed together in Quentin's memory of this episode.

Caddy begins to see Dalton Ames, a stranger in town, and when Mrs Compson hears of it she sets Jason to spy on them. Mr Compson hears of the spying and angrily forbids it. With characteristic self-pity, Mrs Compson complains about her life in general and about the fact that the family does not know the boy Caddy is seeing. On the evening of this day, Quentin explains to his father that he was not the one who had spied upon Caddy as his mother had implied. Mr Compson apologises to him and blames the incident upon the ways of women. Quentin says that his mother acts as though Caddy had already sinned, and his father replies that Quentin is confusing sin and morality whereas his mother is concerned only with morality. Quentin wonders whether his mother's behaviour is related to the fact that her family, the Bascombs, is lower on the social scale than the Compsons.

On the day that it happens, Quentin learns, through Benjy's reactions, of Caddy's loss of her virginity. It happens on an afternoon when the family is sitting together and Caddy walks quickly into the house. Benjy begins to howl immediately upon seeing her standing in the doorway. He smells the difference and pushes Caddy towards the bathroom, wanting her to wash away her changed condition as she had washed away her perfume once before. Mrs Compson lies on a chair downstairs with a camphor-scented handkerchief held to her nose and with Mr Compson holding her hand. Quentin goes to sit on the steps outside the house and sees the streetlights stretching into town. He hears Caddy weeping in her bedroom. When Caddy comes downstairs, T.P. is feeding Benjy who cries again as soon as he sees her. When she touches him he begins to howl. Caddy runs down to the stream and sits in it. Quentin follows her and tries to persuade her to get out of the water. He produces a knife and suggests killing Caddy and then committing suicide. Caddy wants to know if Quentin can do it alone, and although he puts the knife to her throat, when Caddy refuses to touch the blade, he drops it.

Caddy then tells Quentin to go back to the house because she is going to meet Dalton Ames, but they walk together along the ditch where the bones of Nancy the mare lie. Quentin tries to persuade her not to keep her appointment with Ames. They meet him together, and with one hand Ames lifts Caddy to kiss her while shaking hands with Quentin. At Caddy's insistence, Quentin walks back to the stream and when Caddy joins him later and offers herself to him, he tells her to shut up. Shortly after this incident, Quentin sees Ames outside the barber's shop in town and arranges to meet him on the bridge over the stream at one o'clock. On the bridge Quentin tells Ames that he must leave town by sundown, threatens to kill him and tries to slap him but has his hands held by Ames, who remains calm. Ames removes bark from the rail of the bridge, throws it into the river and shoots it very accurately with a pistol which he then offers to Quentin. Quentin faints, recovers, and asks whether Ames had struck him. Ames replies that he had, and then leaves. Caddy, who has followed Quentin and heard the shots, tells Ames that he must never speak to her again, but when she sees that Quentin is all right, wants to follow Ames and apologise to him. Quentin restrains her, and when he asks her whether she loves Ames she tells Quentin to feel the blood surging at her throat when he mentions Ames's name.

Mrs Compson learns of her daughter's affair and wants to go away with Jason. Mr Compson suggests that she takes Caddy to the resort town of French Lick instead, and Mrs Compson, thinking that she might find her daughter a husband there, agrees.

Quentin confesses to his father that he has committed incest with Caddy, and that Dalton Ames was not involved. Mr Compson tells his son that he knows he is still a virgin, that Quentin is too serious for his threat of suicide to worry his father, and that what Quentin really hopes is that by saying that he has committed incest he will thereby make it true. He suggests that Quentin should holiday for a month in Maine before going on to take up his place at Harvard University.

(5) The announcement of the wedding
In his room at Harvard, Quentin leaves the formal announcement of Caddy's forthcoming wedding to Herbert Head lying unopened on a table. He thinks of it as a coffin. Shreve Mackenzie, Quentin's room-mate, jokes with him about not opening it. They quarrel and Quentin is tempted to hit Shreve.

(6) Quentin meets Herbert Head (1910)
Quentin arrives in Jefferson two days before Caddy's wedding and meets Herbert in the car which Herbert has bought for Caddy. Caddy is driving as Mrs Compson boasts that her daughter is the first woman driver in town and that Herbert has promised to find Jason a job in his bank. In the library back at the Compson house, Quentin angrily tells Herbert that he knows about his cheating at cards and during the mid-term examinations, for which Herbert was expelled from Harvard University. Herbert offers Quentin money and then Caddy comes in. She makes Herbert leave the room and then tells Quentin not to meddle in her affairs. Describing him as a blackguard, Quentin protests that Herbert is a scoundrel and a cheat.

(7) The eve of the wedding (23 April 1910)
In her bedroom Caddy asks Quentin to look after Benjy and their father. She explains that she has to marry someone because she is sick, and asks Quentin to promise not to allow Benjy to be taken to the lunatic asylum at Jackson. Quentin blames Caddy for the present circumstances, including their father's increasingly heavy drinking. He tries to embrace Caddy and is told not to. Pressed about her sickness, Caddy replies that she must get married. Quentin wants to know how many lovers she has had and persists in trying to make Caddy say openly that she is pregnant. He wants her to say it to their father. Quentin suggests using his university money for them to run away together, and Caddy refuses.

(8) The wedding (24 April 1910)
Quentin remembers only that during the reception Benjy began to bellow outside the window, and this instantaneously causes Caddy to run out to him, followed by Quentin himself and Mr Compson.

(9) The present, Quentin's final day (2 June 1910)
At Harvard University, Quentin wakes up to the sound of his watch ticking and to memories of his father's thoughts about time. He hears his fellow student Shreve Mackenzie waking and moving about in the next room. Shreve comes in and asks Quentin whether he intends to miss another lesson that morning. Shreve leaves and Quentin looks out of the window to see another fellow student, Spoade, walking towards morning prayers in the chapel. Quentin then watches a sparrow on his window-sill. Thinking of his own suicide, he breaks the face and hands of his watch, cutting his thumb, to which he applies disinfectant. He packs his trunk, leaving out clothes for himself and clothing to give to Deacon, the university's black porter. He bathes, shaves, dresses, and then he addresses an envelope to his father and seals the trunk-key inside. He writes two letters and seals them in envelopes before stepping out of his room into sunlight.

Shreve returns from chapel and Quentin tells him that he is going for breakfast. At the post office Quentin sends a letter to his father and puts the letter to Shreve in his pocket. He then travels across Boston by streetcar in order to eat breakfast at a restaurant called Parkers. After breakfast he buys a cigar and walks past a jeweller's shop, looking away to avoid seeing the watches on display in the window. Passing on he gives two bootblacks money and his cigar before returning to the jeweller's to enquire about the repair of his watch. Told by the jeweller that none of the watches in the window shows the correct time, Quentin feels able to go outside and look at them, noticing in particular one whose hands are almost in a horizontal position. In a hardware store Quentin buys two six-pound flat-irons to serve as weights in his suicide, and then catches a streetcar to return. He sits next to a black passenger and thinks about the relationships between races. He also remembers a train journey home during a Christmas vacation when he joked with a Negro who had stopped by the side of the railway track. The streetcar stops at a swing bridge over the Charles River and Quentin gets off. He watches another student, Gerald Bland, go boating on the river. He recalls another occasion when Bland went boating during winter watched by his mother, and this leads him to think about Mrs Bland at some length, and about how much he dislikes both her and her son for their showy vulgarity. Quentin then catches another streetcar back to the university where he sees Spoade and eventually finds Deacon. Quentin tells Deacon to deliver on the following day a letter which instructs Shreve to give Deacon clothing. Quentin then sees Shreve who tells him that a letter from Mrs Bland is waiting for him. It later transpires that the letter is an invitation to a picnic.

Catching another streetcar, Quentin heads out towards the country. When he arrives at the interurban station, he discovers that he has just missed a connection and so, in order to escape from the sound of the noon whistles from factories, he catches another streetcar instead. Once he is certain that noon has passed, he returns to the station and catches an interurban car. His mind wanders again to Mrs Bland and how she had once tried to move Shreve out so that Quentin could have a room-mate she considered more appropriate. Quentin alights hungry and sees a man eating from a paper bag; he notices a tall factory chimney. He walks to the river, arrives at a stone bridge, hides the flat-irons and stares into the water, watching a trout.

Three boys arrive to fish in the river, and, after talking to them for a while, Quentin walks towards the town. Two of the boys go for a swim while the third walks with Quentin before setting off on his own. Quentin goes into a baker's shop to buy buns and there meets a little Italian girl whom he calls sister. He defends the little girl against the shopkeeper's charge of theft, and also buys her a bun. In another shop, a drug-store, Quentin buys the girl ice cream. The girl then follows Quentin, refusing to leave him. Returned to the town centre, Quentin asks two men for help and they suggest that he finds Anse, the marshal. Having failed in this, Quentin takes the girl to where the Italian community lives in run-down houses near the river, and continues looking for her parents. Unsuccessful again, he tries to escape from the girl by running along a lane, only to find her waiting for him when he climbs over a wall. Together they walk back along the river to where the boys are swimming naked, and are approached by the marshal, Anse, and the girl's brother Julio who attacks Quentin and accuses him of assaulting his sister. At this Quentin laughs hysterically, but has to go back to the marshal's office. Outside the drug-store Quentin sees Shreve, Spoade, Gerald, and his mother Mrs Bland, together with two young ladies. Quentin has to pay a fine of six dollars and he gives Julio a further dollar. In the motor car as the friends drive away, Quentin again laughs uncontrollably. At the picnic area, Gerald Bland begins to boast about his treatment of women and on an impulse Quentin tries to hit him. He doesn't manage to land a blow, but Gerald blacks his eye and bloodies his mouth. Nearby, Shreve and Spoade help Quentin to wash away some of the blood and Quentin insists upon returning to the university alone. He catches the inter-urban trolley and then changes to a streetcar, staying at the back of the carriage so that his damaged face will not be seen by other passengers. The streetcar recrosses the river and Quentin alights before the post office is reached, to walk back to his dormitory room. He changes clothes, putting on the ones he had left for Deacon, and cleans the blood off his waistcoat with petrol. He places his broken watch in a drawer in Shreve's room, brushes his teeth in the bathroom, and then returns to Shreve's room to brush his hat before leaving.

As in the first (Benjy's) section of the novel, Quentin's mind frequently changes backwards and forwards between the episodes summarised above. These changes of episodes are usually indicated in the novel by changes from normal to *italic* type. But the *italics* included by Faulkner do not offer a safe guide to all the changes of scene. The list of episode changes which follows here does offer a precise guide to the different paths taken by Quentin's mind and body. The list gives the first words of each part in normal or *italic* type followed by a note of the episode each of those parts concerns. Not all of the episodes listed are summarised above, so in order to follow the details of the changes, you should read the list with the text of the novel open in front of you.

When the shadow of the sash — present
She ran right out of the mirror — Caddy's wedding
Mr and Mrs Jason Richmond Compson announce — wedding announcement
I said I have committed incest — Caddy's loss of virginity
Shreve stood in the door — present
Calling Shreve my husband — quarrel with Spoade
Because it means less to women — Caddy's loss of virginity
And Shreve said — quarrel with Spoade
Spoade was in the middle — present
I have committed incest — Caddy's loss of virginity
And I will look down and see — considers death by drowning
Dalton Ames. Dalton Ames — Caddy's loss of virginity
One minute she was standing — Caddy's wedding
I went to the dresser — present
Only she was running already — Caddy's wedding
Shreve said, 'Well you didn't' — present
But I thought at first — train journey home, Christmas vacation
I wouldn't begin counting — a day in school
Moving sitting still — childhood scene with Natalie
One minute she was standing — Caddy's loss of virginity
I'm going to run away — Damuddy's death
He smell what you tell him — Benjy is renamed
The streetcar stopped — present
Benjy knew it when — Damuddy's death
The tug came back — present
Did you ever have a sister — Caddy's loss of virginity
And after a while I had been hearing — present
Harvard my Harvard boy — Quentin meets Herbert
That pimple faced infant — Caddy kisses a boy
He was lying beside the box — Caddy's wedding

That could drive up in a limousine — Quentin meets Herbert

Mr and Mrs Jason Richmond Compson announce — wedding announcement

Country people poor things — Quentin meets Herbert

Jason furnished the flour — Jason as a child, already money-seeking

There was no nigger — present

We have sold Benjy's — Mr Compson sells the pasture

He lay on the ground — Caddy's wedding

A brother to you — birth of Benjy

You should have a car — Quentin meets Herbert

Father I have committed — Caddy's loss of virginity

Don't ask Quentin — Quentin meets Herbert

My little sister had no — Caddy's loss of virginity

Unless I do what I am tempted — Quentin meets Herbert

A face reproachful — Caddy's loss of virginity

Hats not unbleached — present

I wouldn't have done — Caddy's loss of virginity

Trampling my shadow's bones — present

I will not have my daughter spied on — Caddy's loss of virginity

The chimes began — present

Think I would have — Caddy's loss of virginity

I walked upon the belly — present

Feeling father behind me — Caddy's loss of virginity

He was coming along — present

Lying on the ground — Caddy's wedding

The street lamps — Caddy's loss of virginity

The chimes ceased — present

Go down the hill — Caddy's loss of virginity

Jason ran on — Damuddy's death

Rolling his head in the cradle — birth of Benjy

Shreve was coming — present

The street lamps — Caddy's loss of virginity

The car came up and stopped — present

Your mother's dream for — Mr Compson sells the pasture

What have I done to have been given — Caddy's loss of virginity

If that was the three quarters — present

Father said a man is the sum — Caddy's loss of virginity

I could hear my watch — present

Who would play — image of death

Eating the business of eating — present

Dalton Ames oh Asbestos — Caddy's loss of virginity

Something with girls — present (Mrs Bland)

Always his voice above the gabble — eve of wedding

Women do have . . . an affinity — present (Mrs Bland)

Quentin has shot — Caddy's loss of virginity
Tone of smug approbation — present (Mrs Bland)
The curtains leaning in on — eve of wedding
The voice that breathed o'er Eden — Caddy's wedding (Benjy's howl)
What he said? Just seventeen — present (Mrs Bland)
Are you going to look after — eve of wedding
Wondered who invented — present
Shot him through the — Caddy's loss of virginity
I saw you come in here — eve of wedding
Shot his voice through the — Caddy's loss of virginity, and eve of wedding
Now and then the river — present
That blackguard Caddy — eve of wedding
The river glinted — present
I'm sick you'll have to promise — eve of wedding
The car stopped — present
There was something terrible in me — eve of wedding
I could see the smoke stack — present
The street lamps go down the hill — Caddy's loss of virginity
You've got fever — eve of wedding
Then they told me the bone — Quentin remembers the pain of his broken leg caused by falling from a horse
At least I couldn't see the smoke stack — present
Told me the bone — Quentin's broken leg
Even sound seemed to fail — present
Niggers. Louis Hatcher — Quentin remembers talking to Louis years ago about a severe flood
I got plenty light for possums — another memory, this time of Quentin hunting possums with Louis and Versh
Got to marry somebody — eve of wedding
I began to feel the water — present
Versh told me about — memory of a story of castration
And father said it's because — Caddy's loss of virginity
Where the shadow of the bridge — present
If it could just be a hell — imagines a purified existence with Caddy
The arrow increased — present
Only you and me — imagines a purified existence with Caddy
The trout hung — present
Caddy that blackguard — eve of wedding
Their voices came over — present
Why must you marry — eve of wedding
Let's go up to the mill — present
Say it to father — eve of wedding
'Ah, come on,' the boy said — present

It is because there is nothing else — Caddy's loss of virginity
He paid me no attention — present
That blackguard Caddy — eve of wedding
Do you like fishing better — present
Caddy that blackguard — eve of wedding
The boy turned from the street — present
Else have I thought about — eve of wedding
Some days in late August — present
But now I know I'm dead — eve of wedding
The buggy was drawn — present
On what on your school money — eve of wedding
His white shirt — present
Sold the pasture — Mr Compson sells the pasture
When you opened the door — present
Seen the doctor yet — eve of wedding
Because women so delicate — Caddy's loss of virginity
You'd better take your bread — present
Getting the odour of honeysuckle — Caddy's loss of virginity
We reached the corner — present
What did you let him for kiss kiss — Caddy kisses a boy
The wall went into shadow — present
Not a dirty girl like Natalie — childhood scene with Natalie
She walked just under — present
I bet I can lift you up — childhood scene with Natalie
We went on in the thin dust — present
It's like dancing sitting down — childhood scene with Natalie
The road went on — present
I hold to use like this — childhood scene with Natalie
We began to hear the shouts — present
Stay mad. My shirt — childhood scene with Natalie
Hear them in swimming — present
Mud was warmer in the rain — childhood scene with Natalie
They saw us from the water — present
We lay in the wet grass — childhood scene with Natalie
There's town again sister — present
And the water building — childhood scene with Natalie
Then we heard the running — present
Ever do that have you — Caddy's loss of virginity
They do, when they can get it — present
Her knees, her face looking — Caddy's loss of virginity
'Beer, too,' Shreve said — present
Like a thin wash of lilac — Caddy's loss of virginity
You're not a gentleman — present
Him between us until — Caddy's loss of virginity

No. I'm Canadian — present
Talking about him — Ames and Spoade become one in Quentin's mind
I adore Canada — present
With one hand he could lift her — Caddy's loss of virginity
Neither did I — present
I don't know too many — Caddy's loss of virginity
And Gerald's grandfather — present (Mrs Bland)
We did how can you not know — Caddy's loss of virginity
Never be got to drink wine — present
Did you love them Caddy — eve of wedding
One minute she was standing — Caddy's loss of virginity
It kept on running for a long time — present
The first car in town — Quentin meets Herbert
It took a lot of gasoline — present
Seeing on the rushing darkness — Quentin sees himself travelling back
  to the bridge to commit suicide
I turned out the light — present
After they had gone upstairs — Caddy's loss of virginity
When I was little — Quentin's mind wanders back to childhood
Then the honeysuckle got into it — Caddy's loss of virginity
Hands can see — present (Quentin's eyes are closed)
It was empty too — present (Quentin is in the bathroom)
Hands can see cooling — present (Quentin brushes his teeth with his
  eyes closed)
Aren't you even going to open it — wedding announcement
I am. Drink. I was not — past and present mix in Quentin's mind
As soon as she came in — Caddy's loss of virginity
Staying downstairs even — Quentin recalls the blacking of Uncle
  Maury's eye by Mr Patterson. He then remembers his ancestors
The three-quarters began — present
And we must just stay awake — Quentin remembers a long conversa-
  tion with his father
The last note sounded — present

NOTES AND GLOSSARY:
mausoleum: burial place
reducto absurdum: incorrect Latin, intended to mean the lowest point
  of absurdity
Good Saint Francis . . . Little Sister Death: Quentin is quoting from the
  Hymn of Saint Francis called the 'Canticle of the
  Sun'. The hymn is a simple song in praise of life
the boat-race: an annual event at Harvard University
New London: a town in Connecticut where Caddy and Herbert
  go for their honeymoon

the month of brides: June
taking a cut: missing a lesson
sluts: women of dirty appearance
terrapin: tortoise
Thompson's: a restaurant
quad: quadrangle, a square of ground
quit swapping eyes: stopped blinking each eye in turn
the day when He says Rise: the Day of Judgement
iodine: chemical used for medicinal purposes
stoop: raised platform before the entrance to a building
the voice that breathed o'er Eden: first line of a marriage hymn by John Keble (1792–1866), which refers to the voice of God during the Creation
cuirass: a piece of armour for the body
Decoration Day: day of remembrance for those who died in the American Civil War
G.A.R.:   Grand Army of the Republic, the army of the Northern States of America
Columbus: discoverer of America (?1451–1506)
Garibaldi: Italian patriot and hero (1807–82)
stove-pipe hat: tall, cylindrical hat
bootblacks: those who black and polish shoes for a living
nickel: coin of American currency, a five-cent piece
derby: stiff felt hat, narrow-brimmed
roman candles: fireworks
scuffed: worn by treading
Benjamin the child of mine old age: in the Bible, Joseph was sold into Egypt and Benjamin was held hostage for Joseph. Faulkner uses them interchangeably. See the Bible, Genesis 37–45
fo'c'sle: forecastle, the raised, forward part of a ship
tailor's goose: smoothing iron
shearing: cutting away
shell: light, narrow racing boat
sculls: type of oars
flannels: white sporting trousers
floes: lumps of floating ice
Oxford Students: students at the University of Oxford, England
Kentuckian: person from the state of Kentucky, USA
noblesse oblige: noble birth imposes the obligation of high-minded principles
Mason and Dixon: the Mason and Dixon line is usually regarded as the boundary between the Northern and Southern States of America

Maingault, Mortemar: names of ancient aristocratic families
no holds barred . . . discretionary: with absolutely no exception
Dalton Shirts: a fashionable style in the South at this time
papiermâché: paper pulp shaped by moulding
celluloid: in this context, artificial
drummer: travelling salesman
Lochinvar: hero of a ballad by Sir Walter Scott (1771–1832), who rescues his lady by carrying her away on horseback from the wedding feast as she is about to marry someone else
Byron never had his wish: 'I wish . . ./That womankind had but one rosy mouth/To kiss them all at once from North to South.' Verse 27, Canto VI of *Don Juan*, by George Gordon, Lord Byron (1788–1824)
darkies: term for Negroes, once considered to be relatively polite
found not death at Salt Lick: Quentin means to say French Lick, where Caddy found her husband
impervious: through which no way can be found
makes a crop: completes the cycle from planting to successful harvesting
fertilizing: making fruitful
Uncle Tom's Cabin outfit: clothing fit for impoverished slaves, ragged and of poor quality. *Uncle Tom's Cabin* (1852) is a novel by Mrs Harriet Beecher Stowe (1811–96), in which the main character is a black slave called Uncle Tom
subjugated: controlled
ubiquitous: present everywhere
garrulous: talkative
raiment: clothing
Brooks: famous American retailer of clothing
Princeton club: a society at Princeton University; the hat-band identifies the particular club
Abe Lincoln: Abraham Lincoln (1809–65), President of the USA during the American Civil War
chicanery: dishonesty
Wop: abusive term for Italian
W.C.T.U.: Women's Christian Temperance Union
Democrat: member of one of America's two main political parties, the other being Republican
claptrap: useless nonsense
confer: a mistake for defer, meaning to give way to
benignant: in a kindly manner

suttee:	the Hindu custom whereby a widow throws herself to die on her husband's funeral pyre
Semiramis:	a beautiful and wise Syrian symbol of fertility, she tricked her king into making her queen for five days, then killed him and ruled in his place. She built the city of Babylon
interurban trolley:	electric streetcar linking different towns
kimono:	Japanese robe with wide flowing sleeves
pumpkin:	large, round or egg-shaped fruit
Confederacy:	the group of Southern States which decided to break away from union with the North
proctor:	university officer in charge of discipline
matriculate:	enrol as a student
Havana:	capital city of Cuba
Dramat:	student drama society
hicks:	stupid persons
Galahad:	a noble knight at the legendary court of King Arthur
gabfest:	conversation
bubber:	brother
see you in the funny paper:	a catch-phrase meaning 'I'll be seeing you'
canaille:	(*French*) the rabble, mob
adulant:	basely flattering
under leather:	when saddled
cur:	mongrel dog
New England:	North Eastern region of USA
chimaera:	monster in Greek mythology
ridge-pole:	roof-supporting timber of a house
aihy:	any
nits:	head lice
coal oil:	kerosene
lichened:	covered with moss
he went into the woods . . . not looping:	refers to a self-inflicted act of castration
then I could say O That That's Chinese:	that is, then I could claim to know nothing about sexuality
mayflies:	winged insects
a sure enough factory:	a real factory (not simply a mill)
cupola:	dome forming the roof or part of the roof of a building
apotheosis:	transformation into a god
chub:	a kind of fish
progenitive:	able to produce offspring

philoprogenitive: loving one's offspring
sent to Coventry: treated with total silence by one's fellows
gauged: measured
desiccating: drying out thoroughly
kike: abusive term for Jew
bunch of switches: an instrument for punishing schoolchildren
taffy: toffee
buggy: a horse-drawn carriage
delicate equilibrium . . . balanced: reference to the menstrual cycle in women
frock coat: a skirted overcoat
façade: front of a building
ammonia: strong-smelling gas
heterogeneous: composed of diverse elements
flags: paving stones
No Spika: that is, I do not speak English
defunctive: dying away
wood-lot: place for storing wood
town-squirt: person fond of showy display
calf-rope: when a child says this he or she admits defeat
cowface: term of abuse
hog-wallow: place where hogs bathe in stinking mud
sloughed: removed
materializing: appearing
Cap: abbreviated form of Captain
squire: justice of the peace
plat: flat area
roach: a wave of hair
congregational: a Christian sect
da pape: immigration papers
fiddlesticks: nonsense
Yankees: nickname for New Englanders
nefarious: wicked
Euboeleus: Faulkner almost certainly intends Quentin to refer to Eubuleus, a god in Greek mythology who was often depicted as a swineherd. According to legend, the swine of Eubuleus were swallowed up at the same time as Proserpine was carried away by Hades, the god of the underworld
crotchety: over-particular; fussy
julep: sweetened and flavoured alcoholic drink
Benjy's the natural: that is, Benjy's the idiot
butt: handle
through a piece of coloured glass: that is, Quentin has fainted

feet bunch scuttering: gravel flies as the horse's hooves come to a halt
son of a bitch: a term of abuse
Mike: the owner of a gymnasium
innuendo: indirect suggestion
Leda . . . the swan: in Greek mythology, Leda was seduced by Zeus, the father of the gods, in the form of a swan
licked: beaten
Wistaria: flowering climbing shrub
brothel: a place of prostitutes
cavalier: a gallant gentleman
gasolene: petrol
throne of contemplation: a jocular term for a lavatory
moses rod: the rod with which Moses struck a rock to produce a flowing stream for the thirsty Israelites. See the Bible, Numbers 20:7–11
Non fui. Sum. Fui. Non sum: (*Latin*) I was not. I am. I was. I am not
the blind immortal boy: in Roman mythology, Cupid, the winged messenger of love
the swine untethered . . . into the sea: Christ cast out devils from a man possessed; the devils entered a herd of swine which then ran violently into the sea. See the Bible, Luke 8:26–36
sublimate: raise to a high degree of purity
exorcise: purify
the dark diceman: the Angel of Death
willy-nilly: whether one likes it or not
Cambridge: a town in the state of Massachusetts
Maine: a state in New England
arbiter: judge

April Sixth, 1928

Jason relates his thoughts and deeds of April Sixth, 1928. He talks to his mother about the unsatisfactory behaviour of Miss Quentin, who often stays away from school and has lied to Mrs Compson about her report card. Jason mocks his mother's suggestions and demands to be allowed to control Miss Quentin himself. Mrs Compson is reduced to tears. Jason finds Miss Quentin in the kitchen, and drags her fiercely into the dining-room. He is about to beat her when Dilsey arrives to restrain him. Hearing his mother coming, he releases Miss Quentin, who runs away upstairs.

Luster has been looking after Benjy and has not replaced the spare wheel on Jason's car. Jason sets off for his job in the hardware store, taking Miss Quentin to school on the way. She believes that her mother has paid for her clothing, and threatens to rip her dress off when Jason tells her otherwise. Furiously he restrains her, leaves her at school, and warns her about her conduct. He arrives at his work, picking up the Compsons' mail on the way. There is a letter from Caddy, containing the cheque which she sends Mrs Compson every month for her daughter Miss Quentin's benefit. Jason puts the letter away and works briefly.

With a travelling salesman, he discusses the cotton market, then goes to the telegraph office to check on the progress of his own investments in cotton. He sends a telegram to Caddy, reassuring her about Miss Quentin, then returns to the store, reads a letter from his mistress Lorraine, thinks about money for a while, and eventually serves a customer. The store is busy with people in town for the show, and Jason cannot find time to read Caddy's letter to Miss Quentin. He reflects self-pityingly on his life, and recalls his father's funeral and the behaviour of his mother and Uncle Maury on that occasion.

Jason goes on to remember that, after Caddy's separation from her husband Herbert Head, Mr Compson went north to bring home her baby daughter, Miss Quentin. Mrs Compson forbade anyone ever to mention Caddy's name again, and refused to allow Miss Quentin to be put to bed in her mother's 'contaminated' room. Dilsey reassured Mrs Compson, put Miss Quentin to bed, and promised to raise her herself, as she had the other children. Mr Compson was not well, but continued drinking as much as ever, despite his doctor's advice.

Jason's recollections switch back to his father's funeral, and the details of his burial. Uncle Maury continued drinking even at the funeral, although he tried to hide the smell of drink on his breath. Jason has received a letter from Uncle Maury. He continues to remember how Maury and Mrs Compson left him in the graveyard, while he watched his father's grave being filled up. After the other mourners had left, Caddy appeared. She had seen a notice of her father's death in a newspaper, and returned with flowers. Because of Caddy's separation from Herbert Head, Jason lost his chance of a job in his bank, and he still bitterly resented this.

Caddy offered Jason fifty dollars if he would let her see her daughter. Eventually he agreed to do so for a hundred. He returned home in a carriage, distracted Dilsey, and removed Miss Quentin. Waiting at a street corner, Caddy saw her daughter only for a second as Jason drove by, holding her up to the carriage window. Furious, she came to Jason's store next morning to protest. He insisted she left town, and took steps to ensure that she would never see her daughter again. In spite of him, she once did so. But Jason cruelly increased his restrictions, despite her pleas, so that in the end Caddy was forced to agree to send money for her daughter's welfare. In fact, Jason has always cheated Caddy. When her cheque for two hundred dollars comes every month, he cashes it himself, and passes on to his mother a forged cheque, knowing that she will always burn this for the sake of her idea of family honour.

Jason is brought back to the present by his boss, Earl, suggesting he eat lunch in town. Left alone, he opens Caddy's letter to Miss Quentin, and finds in it a money order for fifty dollars. Just as Jason is preparing to forge the cheque that he will give to Mrs Compson, Miss Quentin comes into the store, demanding her mother's letter. When Jason serves a customer, she takes it herself. Jason roughly seizes it from her. She pleads with Jason for the money, but he agrees to give her only ten dollars, and forces her to sign the money order over to him.

Jason has run out of the blank cheques he uses to cheat Caddy. Ignoring Earl's instructions, he goes out to look for more, eventually finding some. He prepares one, and seals it up again in Caddy's letter. Before going home for lunch, he stops at the telegraph office and is angered by news of the cotton market. At home, he makes his mother burn the forged cheque as usual. He complains about lunch being late; about his mother's treatment of Miss Quentin; and about Benjy, who he says ought to be sent to the asylum in Jackson. Mrs Compson is upset. He makes her read out Uncle Maury's letter to him, which, as usual, is begging for money. Mrs Compson believes Jason puts his salary in her bank account as an act of generosity. (In fact, Jason uses her account as a way of cashing Caddy's cheques.) She worries that the hardware business is not ideal for him. Jason takes her bank book, deposits money at the bank, and returns to work, after visiting the telegraph office and learning bitterly of the money he is losing on the cotton market.

At the store, he argues with Earl, who suspects that he is cheating his mother. Jason thinks angrily about Earl's interference, and about the Compson family. He goes to the back of the shop, argues about the travelling show with the Negro, Job, who works there, and then sees Miss Quentin. She has left school early and is walking past the store with a showman who wears a red tie. Still thinking bitterly of the madness of his family, Jason pursues them, receiving on the way a telegram telling him of his losses on the cotton market. Feeling cheated, he returns furiously to the store and tells Earl he is going home.

On the way, he thinks about how unpleasant driving is: the smell of petrol gives him a headache. At home, he meets his mother, who is anxious about his welfare and his headaches. He argues with her again about Miss Quentin, collects some money from his room, and sets off back towards the town. On the way, he sees Miss Quentin and the showman in another car. Infuriated, he chases them, still thinking self-pityingly about his headaches and the injustices of his life. He traces their car to a sideroad, where it has been partly hidden, and begins to search on foot, still in pain from his headache. After an unpleasant walk across the fields, he finds his way back to his car, only to see the showman and Miss Quentin driving off in theirs, blowing the horn mockingly. Jason discovers that they have let the air out of his car tyres. He has to borrow a pump from a farmer before he can return to town.

There he discovers the cotton market has fallen still further. He angrily accuses the telegraph clerk of having failed to inform him. Eventually he returns to the store, argues again with Earl, and retires to the back of the shop, thinking bitterly about marriage and the Compson family in general. Looking at the courthouse clock, he thinks of the flocks of birds that cover it and the rest of the town with their droppings. Earl interrupts his thoughts, and they argue again. Earl is looking for Job, who now reappears with the delivery wagon and gives his opinion of Jason's 'smartness' before departing on his errands. Looking at the wagon, Jason thinks angrily about Benjy, and about the inefficiency of Negroes.

After Earl has locked the shop for the night, Jason goes to buy more pain-killers for his headache, and argues about baseball with the shopkeeper. While driving home, he remembers how Benjy used to come to the gate to look for Caddy, and how he attacked a schoolgirl there and was castrated. At home, Dilsey has been preventing Mrs Compson and Miss Quentin from arguing, and now complains that Jason is late for supper. Jason has been given two tickets for the show, and offers to sell one of these to Luster for five cents. In the end, he burns both to tease Luster, who wants to go but has no money. Dilsey comforts him. Jason goes to the library, and is joined there by Luster and Benjy.

Dilsey announces that supper is ready, but Jason refuses to come and eat until Miss Quentin and Mrs Compson also come to the table. Dilsey fetches them from upstairs. At supper, Jason upsets Miss Quentin by making up a story suggesting that he had not chased her himself that afternoon. Miss Quentin bitterly declares that she has been made what she is by Jason's unkind and unloving treatment of her. She rushes back upstairs. Throughout the meal, Mrs Compson is as proud and selfish as ever, and talks critically about her husband, Miss Quentin, Caddy and Quentin, remembering the misdeeds of each of them in the family's history. Jason makes unpleasant remarks, especially about the unknown identity of Miss Quentin's father.

Mrs Compson now locks Miss Quentin in her room every night, thinking that she studies there. Jason goes upstairs, passing Miss Quentin's silent room, then hearing Benjy snoring. He counts his hidden money, recalls Benjy's castration again, and finally thinks over his family and the cotton market with the same anger, self-pity and bitterness he has shown throughout his day.

NOTES AND GLOSSARY:

a bitch: Jason refers abusively to Miss Quentin

her own flesh and blood: her own family

gobbing paint on her face: thickly spreading make-up

drink myself into the ground: drink too much; or, in this case, kill myself with drink

even a Smith or a Jones: anybody: Smith and Jones are very common names

like she had polished it with a gun rag: shiny, oily, and perhaps dirty, as if it had been polished with a cloth used for cleaning guns

slick-headed jellybeans: worthless but fashionable town boys, with well-oiled hair

devilment: evil

cahy: carry or take

knocking a damn oversize mothball around: playing golf

Old Home week: a week when former inhabitants of a village return for celebrations given for them

a fice dog: a small mongrel dog

Beard's lot: Beard's area of ground, where a tent is being put up for the travelling show

wench: a low woman

cultivators: farming machines used in ploughing or growing crops

uncrating: unpacking

no-count: worthless

boll-weevil: an insect pest which destroys cotton plants

wattermilyuns: watermelons

a speculator's crop: a crop suitable for those wishing to exploit stock-market investments

hot air: lies and nonsense

to whipsaw on the market: to manipulate the stock market

to trim the suckers: to exploit foolish investors

to gin: to remove the seeds of cotton and process the fibres

Armenians: emigrants from the south of Russia, many of whom came to the USA

in the ground: on the spot; aware of what is going on

laying for: waiting to catch

make a killing: make a huge sum of money

it was up two points: the stock-market value of cotton had increased by two units

send it collect: send it so that the person receiving the telegram pays for it

dear daddy:	Lorraine's affectionate way of referring to Jason
Q:	Miss Quentin
a bust in the jaw:	a blow on the jaw
redneck:	a contemptuous name for a farmer, a yokel
hame string:	a leather thong used in fixing a horse collar
airy:	either
you're the doctor:	you know best
grafters:	cheats, political manipulators and thieves
screen hooks:	hooks used for hanging curtains
Sewanee:	a university in the state of Tennessee

stop my clock with a nose spray: commit suicide (?)

geldings:	castrated horses. Jason refers unpleasantly to Benjy, also castrated
clove stems:	Uncle Maury uses cloves to hide the smell of drink on his breath
the sideboard:	where the whisky was kept

a one-armed strait-jacket: that is, something to stop Mr Compson drinking

a hant:	a ghost, very pale

the degenerate ape: mankind

a pallet:	a mattress on the floor
the hack:	a horse-drawn carriage

a different breed of cat: a different type of person

the livery stable:	a stable where horses were kept for hire

give the team a bat; give them a cut: whip the horses to make them speed up

number 17:	a regular train service
ragtag and bobtail:	riffraff; low or ordinary people
an audit:	an official check of accounts
the blanks:	the blank cheques Jason needs for his forgeries
a sweetie:	a boyfriend
all this hurrah:	all this disorder and confusion
a bucket shop:	an office illegally or dishonestly selling stocks and shares
sharks:	shrewd or unfair businessmen
an airtight alibi:	a valid excuse

not Milk street and Honey avenue: not a pleasant place

kinfolks:	family
chary:	suspicious

any more concrete medium than speech: writing

the ultimate solidification of my circumstances: a final arrival at financial security

my note of hand at eight per cent per annum: a promise to repay a debt with eight per cent interest

that circumstance of which man is ever the plaything and sport: death; or any unexpected event

a bonanza: something yielding great interest or profit

we will harvest our own vineyards: we will look after our own affairs

of the first water and the purest ray serene: of the best sort

bedlam: madness or chaos. The word comes from the Hospital of St Mary of Bethlehem, a famous London lunatic asylum used since 1403

I have your power of attorney: Jason is legally allowed to act as his mother's agent in legal or financial matters

helling: rushing

his jaw running off: talking and complaining

two by four: small and unimportant

the Western Union: the telegraph company

a wire: a telegram

hand in glove: working closely together

robbing the state asylum of its star freshman: robbing the state asylum of a promising new 'student', Benjy

blood, I say, governors and generals: Jason refers to the Compson family's descent from noble figures

we'd all be down there at Jackson chasing butterflies: we'd all be mad and in the state asylum at Jackson

Louisville: a large town in the state of Kentucky, on the northern edge of the Southern States of America

spute: dispute

Gayoso or Beale Street: streets in Memphis, Tennessee, at the centre of the town's low life

in cahoots with: working together with

dope: information

dock me: reduce my pay

delta: the large, marshy, cotton-producing area around the mouth of the Mississippi river

a thousand dollars' worth of delicate machinery: Jason's car

a ford: a type of car called after its manufacturer Henry Ford (1863–1947), who pioneered assembly line mass production for his model T of which fifteen million were produced between 1908 and 1928

slewed: skidded

forks: crossroads

little shirt-tail country stores: small and insignificant country stores

shares: a system of land use in which a tenant received only a share of any crop he grew on a piece of land he did not own

beggar lice: the sticky, clinging seeds of a weed

poison oak: a plant which can painfully sting the skin
raising so much hell: causing so much trouble
to play with for a squirt gun: to play with as a water pistol
Prohibition: a law which forbade the manufacture or sale of alcoholic drinks in the USA (1920–33)
a hophead: a drug addict
getting a bellyful of them: getting more than enough of them
peace on earth good will toward all and not a sparrow can fall to earth: Jason quotes from the Bible, Luke 2:14; and Matthew 10:29
a little more lip: more cheek or insulting talk
a scantling: a piece of wood
a headache shot: medicine for a headache
the Yankees: a baseball team
the Pennant: the trophy for the team finishing first in the baseball league
that fellow Ruth: Babe Ruth, a famous baseball player
quoilin: quarrelling
hunkered: squatted
like a porcelain insulator: white, shiny, and hard-looking
whoop-de-do: fuss and confusion
the Great American Gelding snoring away like a planing mill: Benjy (who has been castrated), snoring as loudly as the noise of a sawmill
the fence picket: the fence post

April Eighth, 1928

It is early in the morning on Easter Sunday. Dilsey, now old and slow-moving, steps out of her cabin into cold wind and driving rain, then goes back inside for an overcoat. She walks over to the Compson kitchen and a moment later reappears carrying an open umbrella. She walks over to the woodpile, gathers fuel, and struggles back to light the kitchen stove. Mrs Compson repeatedly calls for her hot-water bottle to be filled. Dilsey painfully climbs the stairs and explains to Mrs Compson that Luster has overslept because of being out late at the show the previous night. Mrs Compson is unsympathetic. Dilsey returns to the kitchen, prepares breakfast, and shouts for Luster. He appears from the cellar, Dilsey scolds him, and tells him to bring in wood. Luster enters, spilling logs, and is told to go and dress Benjy. Dilsey begins to sing as she prepares for baking, and then again hears Mrs Compson repeatedly calling for her. Dilsey goes to the foot of the stairs to hear Mrs Compson complain that Luster has not yet dressed Benjy. Dilsey begins to climb the stairs, but when Mrs Compson then tells her that Benjy has not woken up, she climbs back down, checks the stove in the kitchen, and goes outside to look for Luster who at that moment comes out of the cellar. Luster has been trying to make music out of a saw as a performer had at the show the night before, and he is now told to bring more wood and then to dress Benjy. He returns overladen again since he is anxious to continue his practice at the saw. Luster goes to dress Benjy, the kitchen gets warmer, and Dilsey begins to sing again as she continues to prepare the morning meal. The faulty clock strikes five times, by which Dilsey knows that it is eight o'clock. Luster returns with Benjy, and tells Dilsey that Mrs Compson is still waiting for her bottle. Dilsey fills it and gives it to Luster to take upstairs. Jason's bedroom window has been broken and he has accused Luster of doing it. Dilsey gives Benjy his breakfast and Luster feeds it to him. Dilsey then lays the table in the dining-room and rings the bell for breakfast. Mrs Compson and Jason come down talking about the broken window. Everyone assumes that Miss Quentin is still in her bedroom, and Dilsey, who tells Jason that he makes life unpleasant for everyone, is at first unwilling to obey his orders to bring Miss Quentin down to breakfast since on Sunday mornings she is allowed to lie in bed for a while. Finally Dilsey climbs the stairs to do Jason's bidding. Climbing the stairs is painful for her, and Jason comments to his mother that their Negro servants are all useless.

Dilsey is heard upstairs calling to Miss Quentin and receiving no response, while downstairs Jason and Mrs Compson continue to talk. Jason suddenly realises something, rushes upstairs followed by Mrs Compson, and discovers that Miss Quentin's bedroom door is locked. He roughly seizes the key from his mother, knocks her aside when she tries to take it back, and finally succeeds in opening the door to discover that the room is empty. Mrs Compson immediately suspects suicide and asks Dilsey to look for a suicide note. Jason, though, suspecting the truth, goes to his room where he lifts the floorboards under which he hides his money, and discovers that it is missing. While Dilsey looks after Mrs Compson, Jason telephones the police to report the robbery and then leaves the house without his breakfast to go to the sheriff's office.

In the kitchen Benjy begins to bellow, and Luster quietens him for a while by showing him the fire, then Dilsey comes downstairs and quietens him again. After telling Dilsey that he had seen Miss Quentin the night before escaping by climbing down the tree outside her bedroom window, Luster takes Benjy outside to the cellar to continue practising on the saw. Benjy begins to howl again but quietens when Dilsey, who realises that the idiot can smell that something is wrong, finds them, and gets Benjy ready to go to church. They set off for the Negro church to hear the Reverend Shegog, a preacher from

Saint Louis, deliver the Easter Sunday sermon. With Luster and Frony they walk through the Negro quarter discussing Benjy. Shegog, small and monkey-like, begins his sermon in the manner of white people, but rises to a passionate climax in Negro speech. Benjy sits entranced, and Dilsey is moved to tears. Walking back after the service Dilsey, still weeping, reflects upon her life's experience with the Compson family. She dries her tears, and tells Luster to keep Benjy quiet and away from the house.

Inside the house Dilsey soothes Mrs Compson who has retired to bed, complaining that Miss Quentin has not left a suicide note and that her Bible is out of reach. Dilsey then serves the midday meal to Luster and Benjy. By this time Jason is twenty miles away. Certain that Miss Quentin and her lover have stolen the money, he has failed to get the help of the sheriff, who suspects that most of the money belongs to Miss Quentin anyway. Having filled up the tank of his motor car with petrol, and become angry at the Negro attendant for being slow to inflate one of the tyres with air, Jason has driven for some time thinking in a violently bad-tempered and self-pitying way about what might happen to him on the road. His temper is worsened when he realises that he has forgotten to bring camphor with him, which he needs to ease the severe headaches he gets from petrol fumes. His head is causing him considerable pain. For relief he tries to think of his mistress, Lorraine, but thoughts of the stolen money keep returning. His headache is so extreme that he can hardly see. He catches up with the travelling show at Mottson and struggles with an old man in his efforts to discover the whereabouts of Miss Quentin and her showman friend. He is attacked in turn and is rescued by the timely arrival of the showmaster, who tells him that Miss Quentin and her friend have already left. There is no shop open for him to buy something to relieve the pain in his head which is too severe for him to drive his car back himself, and no train is due to leave for some time. After some difficulty, Jason hires a Negro to drive him back to Jefferson.

At the Compson house the midday meal is finished. Dilsey has sent Luster and Benjy outside to play, but they have returned to the cellar where Luster tries again to make music with the saw. Dilsey finds them and tells Luster to take Benjy out into the sunshine. Outside Luster teases Benjy by taking away the glass bottles from the mound of earth which Benjy pretends is a graveyard. They then go to the pasture where they watch golfers playing. Luster repeats Caddy's name in Benjy's ear and the idiot begins to bellow more loudly. Dilsey calls them in and quietens Benjy in her cabin, holding him and sending for his slipper. In order to keep Benjy quiet, Dilsey agrees against her better judgement to allow Luster to drive him for his Sunday visit to the cemetery, since T.P. is not present. Luster gives Benjy a broken narcissus to hold and they set off for town. Luster breaks the usual and familiar pattern of Benjy's weekly visit by driving the horse and carriage the wrong way around the statue in the town square. This causes Benjy to howl louder than ever before. Jason, now back in town, runs to the carriage, strikes Luster furiously, drives Benjy back around the statue, and so quietens the idiot who is reassured by seeing the town buildings pass him by 'each in its ordered place'.

NOTES AND GLOSSARY:

mangy:	shabby
flac-soled:	off-white in colour, resembling the belly of a fish
moribund:	in a dying condition
dropsical:	diseased and swollen with water
patina:	a film on the surface of an object
gingham:	woven check material
jaybirds:	Negroes in this region believed that jaybirds lived in hell from Friday to Monday. On Monday morning they reappeared on Earth
billets:	kindling wood
avatar:	manifestation of a god
daguerro-types:	forerunners of photographs
arpeggio:	a rapid sequence of musical notes in one direction, usually upward
flaccid:	hanging loosely in wrinkles
dimensioned:	measured
Is which?:	Dilsey asks what the matter is
sacque:	loose gown
stereotyped transience: typically short-lived	
assignation houses: brothels	
bureau:	desk
rouge:	red-coloured cosmetic
tongue and groove planking: wooden boards, usually floorboards, shaped to lock tightly together	
the wire opened:	the telephone connection was made
with each . . . expiration: at each breath	
bang:	a wave or fringe of hair
Saint Louis:	a city in the state of Missouri
utilitarian:	useful
locusts:	kind of trees
sibilant:	with a hissing sound
crêpe paper:	wrinkled paper
Christmas bell . . . collapses: pleated paper decoration which folds flat	
alpaca:	fabric woven from the hair of llamas

I've knowed . . . dan dat: Dilsey implies that God has made use of people who are more 'curious' than Shegog

reft of: bereft, deprived of, without

mummy: dead body preserved from decay by embalming

timbrous: bell-like musical sound

alto horn: wind instrument capable of reaching high notes

whelmed: overwhelmed, washed over by

succubus: evil spirit in female form

soprano: highest singing voice in women

retrograde: in reverse motion

coruscations: sparkling flashes

immolation: sacrificial slaughter of a victim

abnegation: self-denial

de ricklickshun . . . Lamb: remembrance (recollection) of the blood shed by Christ (Lamb) on the cross

Calvary: the hill on which Christ was crucified

annealment: purification by fire

egvice: advice

exhumed: dug out

unplumbed: not measured

wimple: veil

Nigger Hollow: the Negro quarter of town

recapitulant: retelling in a more precise manner

Look like it gwine fair off: the weather looks as though it will improve

stalled: unable to move

choker: choke, the device to increase the flow of petrol to a motor car engine

rear guards of Circumstance: Jason feels that fate is against him

dragging Omnipotence down: pulling God down from heaven

reconnoitred: made observations (of an enemy)

tenor: male voice between the bass and the alto

wasp: an angry person

ravelled: unspun and frayed out

barrel-staves: narrow pieces of wood slightly curved to fit together in the shape of the barrel

cheekstrap: part of a horse's harness

narcissus: a white flower frequently symbolising vanity

subterranean rumblings, organlike basso of her internal accompaniment: the aged Queenie is being made to run quickly, and her guts are churning and rumbling in protest

boneyard: graveyard

elefump: elephant

hiatus: an empty space held in suspension

Part 3

Commentary

Introduction: the novelist against time

The title of Faulkner's novel, *The Sound and the Fury*, is taken from the following speech in *Macbeth*, by William Shakespeare:

> Tomorrow, and tomorrow, and tomorrow,
> Creeps in this petty pace from day to day,
> To the last syllable of recorded time;
> And all our yesterdays have lighted fools
> The way to dusty death. Out, out, brief candle!
> Life's but a walking shadow: a poor player,
> That struts and frets his hour upon the stage
> And then is heard no more: it is a tale
> Told by an idiot, full of sound and fury,
> Signifying nothing.
>
> (Act V Scene 5)

Macbeth makes this speech after hearing about the death of his wife, and some of its general feelings about loss, decay and death are present in *The Sound and the Fury*. Details of the passage are also repeated in the novel: for example, the contrast of light with darkness, and the idea of life as 'a walking shadow' occur frequently, especially in the first two sections of the novel. Benjy often notices how his 'shadow walked on the grass'. When Quentin wakes up on June Second, 1910, the first thing he sees is a shadow on the curtains, and he continues to find and watch carefully very many such shadows, and patterns of sunlight and shade, throughout the last day of his life. He seems almost afraid of his own shadow, talking about 'trampling my shadow's bones into the concrete with hard heels', and thinking about the superstition that 'a drowned man's shadow was watching for him in the water all the time'.

Of course, the most obvious point of comparison between Macbeth's speech and Faulkner's novel lies in the idea of life being 'a tale told by an idiot': not only is Benjy an idiot, but Quentin is also mentally disturbed (although highly intelligent), and sometimes even Jason does not seem entirely sane. Many critics have taken the comparison further, and claimed that *The Sound and the Fury* is not only 'a tale told by an idiot', but that it 'signifies nothing'; that it is confusing, disordered and meaningless. The following opinion is typical of such approaches to the novel, suggesting that the reader

> is repelled almost invariably by Faulkner's disposition to tell his stories in a round-about and riddling manner, with the most brazen neglect of chronological sequence, and the most wanton use of every trick for confusing the reader, leading him astray, putting him off, and generally teasing and bewildering him.*

There is no doubt that *The Sound and the Fury* is a 'difficult' novel; one that is not easily read and which may confuse the reader so much that he or she fails to understand what is happening in some parts. The critic quoted above mentions Faulkner's 'neglect of chronological sequence': perhaps it is this, as much as the use of an idiot to tell part of the story, which makes *The Sound and the Fury* so hard to understand. Most novels tell a story from beginning to end, moving constantly forward in time, like history, and describing events or situations one after the other. But Faulkner mixes up the events in the story of the Compson family, and does not present these happenings to us in the order in which we feel they actually occurred. Instead, each of the first three sections of the novel is a confused mixture of a character's awareness of the present, and many of his disordered memories of the past. Worse still, the sections of the novel – 'April Seventh, 1928'; 'June Second, 1910'; 'April Sixth, 1928'; and 'April Eighth, 1928' – are not even arranged in historical order.

In a famous essay, the French novelist and philosopher Jean-Paul Sartre (1905–80) neatly summed up these problems with the novel: 'The first thing that strikes one in reading *The Sound and the Fury* is its technical oddity. Why has Faulkner broken up the time of his story and scrambled the pieces?'† Answers to this question may help to make clear some of the difficulties presented by the unusual and complicated way Faulkner tells his story. One possible answer is suggested a little later in Sartre's essay. He remarks: 'Most of the great contemporary authors, Proust, Joyce, Dos Passos, Faulkner, Gide, and Virginia Woolf, have tried, each in his own way, to distort time'§ Several novels written (or, in Proust's case, translated into English) in the 1920s seemed to give up the order of time, and present their stories in new, and often confusing ways. During this period, both James Joyce (1882–1941) and Virginia Woolf (1882–1941) published novels in which the telling of the story is compressed into one day, or a few days,

*J.W. Beach, *American Fiction 1920–1940*, Macmillan, London, 1941, p.124.
†Jean-Paul Sartre, 'On *The Sound and the Fury*: Time in the Work of Faulkner', reprinted in *Twentieth Century Views of Faulkner*, edited by Robert Penn Warren, Prentice-Hall, New Jersey, 1966, p.87.
§ibid., p.91.

with characters' memories used to fill in the history of their previous lives. Marcel Proust (1871–1922) and John Dos Passos (1896–1970), too, gave up the usual time sequence of telling their stories from beginning to end. Faulkner was probably influenced in writing *The Sound and the Fury* by several of these new experiments in fiction.

It would be quite wrong, however, to suggest that by giving up the usual order of time in telling his story, Faulkner was only following the literary fashion of the 1920s, and unfair to claim that his novel is only a clever but empty experiment – 'full of sound and fury' but 'signifying nothing'. As Richard Hughes said in his introduction to the first English edition of *The Sound and the Fury*, although Faulkner's method is complicated and difficult to follow, it is nevertheless 'the clearest, the simplest, the only method of saying in full what the author has to say'. The reasons for using such an unusual and difficult technique are contained in the story itself, and can best be illustrated by first considering Quentin's section, 'June Second, 1910'.

As soon as Quentin wakes up on June Second he hears the tick of his watch, a family heirloom which his father has passed on to him. Mr Compson described the watch as the 'reducto absurdum of all human experience' (that is, a stupid and useless way of treating life), and explained to his son that 'clocks slay time . . . time is dead as long as it is being clicked off by little wheels; only when the clock stops does time come to life'. Quentin shares his father's belief that mechanical counting of time can distort experience and make it false: life continues by itself, and cannot be defined by clockwork. He even goes so far as to think, 'Christ was not crucified: he was worn away by a minute clicking of little wheels'. Quentin's first action on his last day at Harvard is to break his watch, and for the rest of the day he carefully tries to avoid knowing what time it is. One reason he so often notices shadows and sunlight is that, like sundials, they may suggest to him the time of day.

Part of Quentin's reason for hating and fearing clocks and watches is that he is so hurt by the passage of time. The history of his family has been for him only one of loss: loss of Caddy's innocence, loss of the family honour, and finally the loss of Caddy herself. Quentin is upset by the temporary nature of everything, and by continual change and loss in his experience. He wants to stop time, and remain with Caddy in some eternal and changeless way: 'Finished. If things just finished themselves. Nobody else there but her and me . . . to isolate her out of the loud world . . . the clean flame the two of us more than dead.' But this is impossible. He can find only one final and changeless act, and that is suicide.

Not only in 'June Second, 1910', but throughout *The Sound and the Fury*, time is shown not as a source of order, but as a 'petty pace' which 'creeps in from day to day' and brings gradual ruin and disorder to the decaying Compson family. This is stated most clearly in the last section of the novel: 'The clock tick-tocked, solemn and profound. It might have been the dry pulse of the decaying house itself'. In the Compson household, and perhaps more generally in Faulkner's South, history and the progress of time could no longer be seen as ordered, but rather as an increasing disorder and a decline from a grand, noble past to a confusing and miserable present (see Part 1 of these notes). For example, Jason Compson, senior, is the descendant of 'governors and generals', but his son Jason has to work in a hardware store and steals money from his sister and his niece. The 'scrambled' time of *The Sound and the Fury* reflects the position of the Compsons, and of the South: uneasy in the present, they look back to a happier past, but cannot look forward with certainty to any future. For them, time is no longer a smooth and ordered progress, but a disordered decline.

Sartre's question has been partly answered. Time and history are no longer useful orders for the Compson family, who cannot use clocks and watches to make sense of their confused lives; so Faulkner does not attempt to use the order of time in *The Sound and the Fury*, but 'stops the clock' of the novel and concentrates on the lives of its characters themselves. But once the clock is stopped, what order is left? Without the usual regular forward progress in time, is *The Sound and the Fury* only a confusing collection of 'scrambled pieces'?

The answer is that Faulkner only *seems* to have given up the idea of telling a story and showing the progress of the Compsons' family history. The clock has not really stopped: in subtle ways, the novelist still shows us the passage of time, and presents his story so that order within the novel increases throughout, in several different ways.

Although the sections of the novel are presented 'out of order' ('April Seventh, 1928'; 'June Second, 1910'; 'April Sixth, 1928'; April Eighth, 1928'), the memories of the characters concerned in each of these sections do follow one another in time. Benjy, who has remained 'three years old thirty years', is mentally still a child. In the first section, he mostly remembers what happened to the Compson children when they were young, especially Damuddy's death and the day his name was changed. He also remembers a few incidents concerned with Caddy as she grew up. Quentin, in the second section, mostly remembers what happened when Caddy, now grown up, lost her virginity and later got married. In the third section, Jason usually thinks of the present. His few memories are about what happened after Caddy's wedding, and what has happened to the family since then. The fourth section of the novel mostly concerns Dilsey, who is almost entirely involved with what is happening in the present.

A progress toward order can also be seen by comparing the minds of the characters at the centre of each part of the novel. Benjy is an idiot: the past and the present are really the same in his mind. Anything that happens to him on April Seventh, 1928, may make him return entirely to some event earlier in his life. He does not sort out or arrange his experience at all. For Quentin, like Benjy, the present is so much part of the past that present and past seem almost the same. But although Quentin's disturbed mind sometimes seems nearly out of control, he is intelligent, and his memories are usually associated directly and often logically with what is happening to him in the present. It is easier to understand and follow the events of his day, 'June Second, 1910', than it is to see what is happening on Benjy's day, 'April Seventh, 1928'. Jason is much freer from the past and memories of it than either Benjy or Quentin. He tries to do everything in a completely sane and logical way. Sometimes this determination leads him to act foolishly or almost madly himself, but his section, 'April Sixth, 1928', is much more orderly and coherent than the first two. Dilsey, who has to look after the whole Compson household, is the most sane character in *The Sound and the Fury*, and the fourth section of the novel is straightforward and easy to understand.

Perhaps this progress in order and sanity between the sections of the novel is shown most clearly by the feelings each of the characters has about time itself. Benjy cannot connect past and present logically. He is vaguely aware of the pain of change and loss resulting from Caddy's departure from the household, but has no understanding of time itself, or of clocks. When he burns his hand and bellows in pain, he 'could still hear the clock between [his] voice', but he has no idea of what the ticking means. Quentin's hand is less seriously hurt when he breaks his watch. He has a very clear idea of time, but a very strong urge to escape from it, and the clocks which measure it. Jason's ideas are almost opposite. He lives very seriously and carefully by the clock, often thinks anxiously about the right time (he even worries about cleaning the courthouse clock), and usually records exactly the time of day at which things happen to him. Only Dilsey seems clear-headed and untroubled about time: 'a cabinet clock ticked, then with a preliminary sound as if it had cleared its throat, struck five times. "Eight o'clock," Dilsey said'. Dilsey understands and can make sense even of the inaccurate Compson clock, and is free from anxiety about time. She endures, without worrying about the clock. Her religious belief gives her faith in eternity beyond the worries of the world's time. She 'seed de beginnin, en now . . . sees de endin'.

So although Benjy, Quentin, Jason, and Dilsey's sections of the novel are not placed in the usual order of time, order does increase between them. However, at least the first two sections of the novel seem very confusing, disordered, and difficult to understand in themselves. Why has Faulkner 'scrambled the pieces' within these sections? An answer can be found in the way we experience *The Sound and the Fury*. In reading most novels, it is enough to imagine what is happening to the characters we are being told about. But in the first two sections of *The Sound and the Fury*, we experience this much more directly. We are taken inside the minds of Benjy and Quentin, and, because their disordered thoughts are not sorted out for us by the author, we are forced to make sense of them for ourselves. The Compson family find their history collapsing and confused: they try to reach an understanding of it, and we are made to share this struggle with them completely. We are presented by Faulkner with a disordered history, and have to work out an ordered story for ourselves. As our efforts continue throughout the novel, the story itself becomes clearer. After the more straightforward presentation and direct explanations of the last section, when we no longer experience the mind of an idiot but see objectively what is happening, we can make sense of the confusing parts which have gone before. By the end of *The Sound and the Fury*, things 'flow smoothly once more . . . each in its ordered place'.

So Faulkner's technique of 'breaking up the time of his story and scrambling the pieces' may make his novel confusing and difficult to read, but it should be understood as essential and appropriate to the story he tells. The way the Compson story is told adds to the whole meaning of the story itself. *The Sound and the Fury* partly concerns the struggle to make life ordered, rather than 'full of sound and fury, signifying nothing', and we are not just told about this struggle, we are made to take part in it ourselves. When time and history seem the meaningless 'clicking of little wheels', a better order has to be found, and Faulkner 'scrambles the pieces' in order to find one. By 'stopping the clock' of *The Sound and the Fury*, he allows a different order, a human time, to come to life.

Structure

The story of the Compson family is quite simple and straightforward in itself, but Faulkner's method of telling it is complicated. *The Sound and the Fury* is made up of four very different sections. The first three present events through the minds of characters who take part in those events. In the first section, we learn about 'April Seventh, 1928', through the confused, idiot mind of Benjy. In the second, we learn through his own disturbed mind of Quentin's last day at Harvard, 'June Second, 1910'. The third section, 'April Sixth, 1928', is told through the thoughts of Jason, the sanest but most bitter and unpleasant of the Compson brothers. Apart from an account of Jason's pursuit of Miss Quentin, the last section, 'April Eighth, 1928', mainly concerns Dilsey, and is told directly and objectively by the author. Throughout the novel, Dilsey is shown selflessly trying to bring order to the Compson household, and it is appropriate that the most orderly section of the novel should concentrate on her, rather than on the disturbed Compsons.

The Sound and the Fury seems to present the events of only four days, and on at least two of these, little of importance seems to happen. April Seventh is Benjy's birthday: he wanders around with Luster, is given a cake by Dilsey, and burns his hand. On April Sixth, Jason goes to work, cheats Caddy of money, argues with Miss Quentin, and chases her and her lover – all much as usual. Of course Quentin's day at Harvard, the last of his life, is unique; April Eighth is also unusual and eventful, Jason looking for Miss Quentin in Mottson after finding he has been robbed. However, Faulkner concentrates on these four days not only because of the events that occurred during them, but as a way of presenting a whole history of the Compsons from 1898 to 1928. As pointed out earlier in the Notes, this history is revealed to us, in the first two sections of the novel, through the memories of Benjy and Quentin; in the third (to a lesser extent) it is revealed through that of Jason. We are brought up to date and shown the present state of the Compson household in the fourth section, and in parts of the third.

'April Seventh, 1928' contains Benjy's memories of almost all the major events of the Compson family history. Along with Benjy's lesser recollections, these are listed below in historical order:

Damuddy's death (1898)
Benjy is renamed (1900)
Christmas-time/Uncle Maury's affair
Caddy uses perfume (1906)
Caddy in the swing
Benjy has to sleep alone (1908)
Caddy's loss of virginity (1909)
Caddy's wedding (1910)
Benjy in the garden (1910)
Quentin's death (1910)
Mr Compson's death (1912)
A trip to the cemetery (1913)
Roskus's death

Benjy mostly remembers the earliest episodes, although he does recall Caddy's wedding and his father's death in some detail. Quentin's section, 'June Second, 1910', adds details to several parts of the Compson story that Benjy only introduced. Since Quentin was so involved with Caddy, and most concerned about her affair with Dalton Ames, and her later marriage to Herbert Head, his section concentrates on these episodes, which occurred shortly before his suicide. Jason never seems to recover from his disappointment at losing the chance of a job in Herbert Head's bank, so his mind mostly goes back to the failure of Caddy's marriage, the return of Miss Quentin to the Compson household, the death of his father shortly afterwards, and Caddy's secret visit to Mr Compson's grave. He also remembers what has happened since (between 1912 and 1928), particularly his schemes for cheating Caddy of the money she sends for her daughter.

So the first three sections of *The Sound and the Fury* show us far more than the events of only three days. They show us the past of the Compson family, and provide a history of it. In parts of the third section, and in the fourth, the remaining family appears clearly in the present, 1928. So although the novel's structure may seem confused or careless, it is actually very cleverly constructed in its use of four different days, and its exposition of the points of view of three different characters, and of the author himself, to give a more complete view of the same history. This method of telling the Compson story also gives us a very clear picture of the characters who present it to us. *The Sound and the Fury* not only tells us about the Compson family, but shows, with a wonderful depth of human detail, the unhappy positions of Benjy, Quentin, Jason and Dilsey within its tragic history.

William Faulkner himself made some comments on his use, in writing *The Sound and the Fury*, of four different points of view to tell the same story:

> I tried first to tell it with one brother, and that wasn't enough. That was Section One. I tried with another brother, and that wasn't enough. That was Section Two. I tried a third brother, because Caddy was still to me too beautiful and too moving to reduce her to telling what was going on, that it would be more passionate to see her through somebody else's eyes, I thought . . . and I tried myself – the fourth section – to tell what happened . . . I tried to gather the pieces together and make myself the spokesman.*

Because the author will not 'reduce her to telling what was going on', no section of the novel belongs entirely to Caddy, but the first three sections do concern her directly. Caddy still exists for Benjy as a feeling of painful loss which is set off by very many occurrences, especially the mention of her name. He and Quentin were so fond of Caddy that her loss was the major tragedy of their lives. Quentin's strange thoughts continually return to her. Jason never forgives or forgets her responsibility for his lost job, and directs most of his energy to using her love for her daughter to cheat her of money. Caddy is not quite absent even from the fourth section, for Miss Quentin is shown

***Faulkner in the University*, p.1, and *Writers at Work*: The Paris Review Interviews, edited by Malcolm Cowley, Vol. I, Secker and Warburg, London, 1958, p.118.

to be growing up much as her mother did, and in some ways repeating her history. Because the effects of Caddy's character and actions on the rest of her family are shown so clearly, and in such detail, she seems central to the story of the Compsons in *The Sound and the Fury*.

Style and technique

Faulkner once remarked, 'the style must change, according to what the writer is trying to tell. What he is trying to tell in fact compels the style'.* Because the first three sections of *The Sound and the Fury* present the thoughts of Benjy, Quentin, and Jason, and in the fourth the author 'tries to make himself the spokesman', different styles and methods are used 'according to what the writer is trying to tell' in each. These are considered separately below.

April Eighth, 1928

The language of Benjy's section seems unusual, even on the first page of the novel: 'I could see them hitting . . . they were hitting little, across the pasture . . . Then there was a bird, slanting and tilting on it. Luster threw. The flag flapped on the bright grass and the trees.' Benjy's use of the words 'hit' and 'throw' seems particularly odd. Normally, people hit or throw *something*: Benjy notices only that 'they were hitting' and that 'Luster threw', without including any idea that this hitting or throwing might have been to move an object for some reason. There also seems to be something strange about the way he looks at the flag and the bird. The subjects of his short, simple sentences seem to change constantly and without any reason. On the first page, his attention moves from the golfers to Luster, to himself, to the flag, and to the bird, without suggesting any relationship between them. Benjy seems to record pieces of his experience without connecting these with each other. In particular, he does not connect anything that happens to him with anything that might have caused it to happen. For example, when he is playing with his flowers, he notices that 'Luster picked them up, and they went away', but he does not consider that the flowers have 'gone away' because Luster has removed them, and has done so in order to tease him. When Benjy's mind is on Caddy's wedding, he records only what seems to be happening: 'I ran into the box. But when I tried to climb onto it it jumped away and hit me on the back of the head and my throat made a sound.' He is unable to understand that he has fallen from the box, and is crying in pain because he has hurt himself.

Faulkner once explained that Benjy's mind was 'capable only of

Faulkner in the University, p.279.

knowing what happened, but not why'.* Throughout 'April Seventh, 1928', the reader has to work out (or sometimes guess) what is happening, because Benjy cannot do so for himself. Of course it is impossible to know how an idiot really thinks. But Faulkner's use of simple, unconnected sentences, with abnormal patterns of words within them, creates a language which successfully suggests the strange workings of Benjy's mind. The absence of any reasons for the events which take place adds to this impression.

Because he is unable to sort his experiences even into present and past, Benjy's mind constantly moves about in time. His thoughts do not move from one episode to another logically: they simply change when something happens which makes his mind switch to a similar occurrence. For example, when he crawls through the fence with Luster, his clothes catch on a nail, and his mind immediately returns to the time in his childhood when his clothes caught on a nail as he crawled through the fence. His mind remains more or less on this episode until he remembers the loss of Caddy's love and begins to cry. He is brought back to the present by Luster telling him not to cry so loudly. Soon he sees a carriage, and his mind switches back to a ride to the cemetery fifteen years earlier, and so on.

Faulkner usually indicates these switches in Benjy's attention by changing from normal to *italic* type, or from *italic* back to normal type. Sometimes, there is a change of type which does not indicate a change of episode, and occasionally, when Benjy's mind moves straight from one remembered episode to another without returning to the present at all, there is no change of type to indicate the movement. For example, when Benjy's thoughts about Damuddy's death reach the point where Caddy mentioned the horse Nancy's bones, his mind passes directly to the death of his father. Normal type is used throughout. However, changes of type are usually reliable in suggesting that Benjy's mind has moved from one episode to another, although they do not make clear *which* episode he is remembering. But there are many clues which the reader learns to recognise: for example, since Luster looks after Benjy throughout April Seventh, 1928, we can be fairly sure that if Luster is mentioned, Benjy's thoughts are on the present.

A large part of Benjy's section is taken up with memories of death – the deaths of Damuddy, Nancy, Quentin, Mr Compson and Roskus all follow one another in his mind. He even has a play area called his 'graveyard'. Death brings about change in the Compson family, and takes Benjy away from his happy childhood for ever. Like Quentin, Benjy is afraid of change, and of anything unusual or disordered in his experience. Most of his happier thoughts concern bright, orderly

Writers at Work, p.117.

shapes: the bright grass and trees of the pasture; his mother's shining jewellery box; firelight; the countryside flowing past a moving carriage; and the 'smooth, bright shapes like . . . when Caddy says that I have been asleep'.

Because he has no intelligence, Benjy's thoughts most often concern things which simply please or frighten him – firelight, Caddy, trees, flowers, bright shapes, sleep, and death. These simple, repeated thoughts of love, nature, and death flow together and mix with each other to create in 'April Seventh, 1928' not only a convincing impression of an idiot's mind, but also a strange sort of poetry.

June Second, 1910

As in 'April Seventh, 1928', Faulkner uses *italic* type to indicate parts of the text in which Quentin's mind has slipped away from the present and returned to memories of the past. But these changes are much more frequent than in Benjy's case, since Quentin is highly intelligent and quickly associates complicated thoughts with each other. Benjy's mind usually continues in a past episode until something happens to bring him back to the present. Often Quentin suddenly and very briefly switches back to the past and then returns almost at once to what is happening in the present. For example:

> that quality of autumn always in bells even in the month of brides. *Lying on the ground under the window bellowing* He took one look at her and knew. Out of the mouths of babes. *The street lamps* The chimes ceased. I went back to the post office, treading my shadow into the pavement. *Go down the hill then they rise toward town like lanterns hung one above another on a wall.*

Here the sound of a clock chiming makes Quentin think of bells; of brides; of Caddy's wedding when Benjy lay drunk and bellowing outside the window; of another occasion when Benjy bellowed, sensing that Caddy had lost her virginity; and of how at that time he and his father had talked outside one night, looking at the streetlights on the road into town. These thoughts are intelligently linked to each other, but are very thoroughly mixed with what is happening in the present. Quentin's learning also makes him think in complicated ways. His mind ranges widely on June Second, and it is often difficult to follow.

As his day progresses, his thoughts seem to become more and more disorderly. Eventually, while he fights Gerald Bland, his mind loses hold of the present completely, and passes back for many pages to Caddy's affair with Dalton Ames. Caddy and her sexuality remain so firmly and constantly in Quentin's mind that almost all his thoughts and memories concern her.

Quentin's thoughts, like Benjy's, return frequently to certain objects, remembered or appearing on June Second. It has already been suggested that he keeps noticing shadows, partly because of his constant worries about clocks and time. Since many of the remembered scenes with Caddy took place while they were washing or playing in the stream, and his own day will end in drowning, water also appears often in his thoughts.

April Sixth, 1928

The first two sections of *The Sound and the Fury* are written in a stream-of-consciousness form (see Part 1 of these notes). Jason's section is similar, but he swears, uses slang, and repeats the phrases 'I says', 'he says', 'she says', so often that it sounds almost as if we were overhearing him telling aloud the story of his day. Much of his section is in the form of direct speech, his own and that of other people. Perhaps Jason is only telling his story to himself, but even his private thoughts – for example, 'Once a bitch always a bitch, what I say' – sound as though they were meant to be spoken aloud.

Every part of Jason's life on April Sixth seems to be calculated. The time of day and every move of the stock market are noted exactly. Jason pays particularly precise attention to money. Throughout his section, money and financial matters are referred to very frequently and exactly. He remembers the amount he paid for Miss Quentin's books, mentions how much he gave his mistress Lorraine, records exactly his losses on the stock market, and many other figures besides. Jason bases all his judgements on money values, and he seems so unpleasant partly because so much of his record of April Sixth concerns money and not people. Benjy lacks all reason and intellect, but responds to his experience all the more directly in an emotional way: Jason seems almost the opposite. Although he often seems to act foolishly, he tries hard to behave as logically as possible, and persuades himself he has good reasons for all his actions. But everything he does shows him to be cruel, greedy, selfish, calculating, and almost without any gentle emotions.

The Sound and the Fury contains little humour. However, there are several amusing parts in Jason's section. He always feels so bitter about the way he is treated that he exaggerates the unpleasantness:

I found a nigger and sent him for my car and stood on the corner and waited . . . after about a week he got back with it . . .

I happened to look around and I had my hand on a bunch of poison oak. The only thing I couldn't understand was why it wasn't a snake or something.

Jason is so nasty about other people, feels so self-important, and is so sorry for himself, that he is often carried away into wild and amusing imaginings:

> the first thing I know they're going to begin charging me golf dues, then mother and Dilsey'll have to get a couple of china door knobs and a walking stick and work it out, unless I play at night with a lantern. Then they'd send us all to Jackson, maybe. God knows, they'd hold Old Home week when that happened.

Phrases like 'Once a bitch always a bitch', 'I don't want to make a killing', 'Damn New York jews', occur over and over again. The repetition of these sour ideas; the way Jason's thoughts so often and exactly concern money; the way his self-pity and self-importance lead him to exaggerate any unpleasantness, all give the impression of a bitter man determined to hurt himself as much as anyone else by telling the story of his selfishness on April Sixth, 1928.

April Eighth, 1928

Unlike the first three sections, the fourth section of *The Sound and the Fury* does not show us the mind of a character, or present his thoughts. Instead, we see the characters 'from outside', and learn something about their appearance. For example, Dilsey's clothing is described in detail, and we are told about the 'bullet-like silhouette of Luster's head'. Dilsey is the character about whom we hear most, but her thoughts are never presented directly. She is seen from some distance, and her behaviour and appearance are recorded. The fourth section seems to be told by a careful observer, who stands apart from the action he describes, and occasionally makes judgements about it. For example, Mrs Compson is said to be 'like many cold, weak people'. In the first three sections, we work out from her actions and conversation that she is cold and weak. In the fourth section, this is stated directly.

Faulkner explained that in the fourth section he tried 'to gather the pieces together and make [himself] the spokesman', and we may suppose that the fourth section gives the author's own point of view. Many of his other novels are written in an intense and energetic prose, which often uses odd constructions and strange or difficult words. Some examples of this appear in 'April Eighth, 1928'. In the first paragraph, Faulkner describes Dilsey's face as 'myriad and sunken', and talks of 'somnolent and impervious guts'. Although such choices of words seem unusual, their strangeness adds depth to the description, and makes the reader think more carefully about the object or person described.

Apart from some odd uses of words, the fourth section presents what is happening as clearly and directly as possible, helping the reader to make sense of what has happened in the other sections. For example, the fourth paragraph of 'April Eighth, 1928' contains sentences which begin 'A moment later . . . Immediately . . . Then . . . Then . . . While she was doing so . . .'. All these words refer to the time of the actions which the sentences go on to describe, and show the exact order in which these took place. After the confused time of the first three sections, the fourth does 'gather up the pieces', presenting events as simply as possible and showing how each follows from the one before, 'in its ordered place'.

Although the style of *The Sound and the Fury* varies a great deal from section to section, it would be wrong to assume that the novel lacks unity as a result. Although the operations of three very different minds are shown in the first sections, the Compson brothers do have several characteristics in common. Benjy and Quentin notice shadows and patterns of light very frequently, and all three brothers are sensitive to smells. Benjy remembers most happily how 'Caddy smelled like trees', and seems able to sense death by smelling it, although he cannot understand what it is. Quentin remarks 'Honeysuckle was the saddest odour of all, I think. I remember lots of them'. He associates the smell of honeysuckle with Caddy's sexuality, and so thinks of it very often. He also responds strongly to many other smells, and can even 'smell the curves of the river'. Jason suffers badly from the smell of petrol, and sometimes, like Benjy, 'could almost smell . . . impending disaster'. All three brothers often notice birds. Benjy sees one 'slanting and tilting' above the golf course. Quentin notices a sparrow on his window-sill shortly after waking up, and later watches gulls over the river. Jason records his dislike of the sparrows, pigeons, and swallows whose droppings foul the court-house clock and the centre of Jefferson. Even in the last section, Luster watches jaybirds whirling over the Compson house. As well as showing the differences between his characters' responses, Faulkner uses repeated references like these to create a feeling of unity and continuity in *The Sound and the Fury*.

Negro speech in the Southern idiom also appears throughout the novel. Dilsey, Luster, Frony, T.P., Versh, Roskus and the other black characters all talk in a very different way from the white Compsons. Often their speech is unusual, powerful, and imaginative: the Reverend Shegog's sermon is a good example. Quentin records his feeling that black people 'come into white people's lives in sudden sharp black trickles that isolate white facts for an instant in unarguable truth like under a microscope'. Dilsey's calm and unselfish endurance 'isolates white facts' by contrast with the Compsons' failure and decline. Likewise, throughout the novel, Negro speech is a constant reminder that around the Compsons live another people who are untouched by the sound and the fury of their disordered lives.

Characterisation

With only one exception, none of the characters in *The Sound and the Fury* can be said to show any real development. Benjy grows older in body but otherwise does not change. As a child Jason shows the same self-seeking spitefulness as he does as an adult, and Quentin is disturbed and unstable throughout the novel. The other characters are presented in a similar way. They seem to be frozen in time and their qualities are gradually revealed, but do not really develop. The exception to this way of presenting character is Caddy. The changes which she undergoes do have effects upon many of the rest of the characters in the novel, bringing to the surface aspects of them that are otherwise only hinted at.

As Caddy grows into maturity she moves away from the world of childhood to begin her own life of adult experience. Her commitment to her own life introduces to the Compson family a kind of reality with which they cannot cope. Mr Compson avoids the problem by generalising it as the ways of women, while Mrs Compson uses Caddy's experience as an excuse to indulge in exaggerated feelings of shock, disgust, and self-pity. Benjy's loss of his beloved Caddy removes a centre of love from his deprived life. Jason is able to blame Caddy bitterly for his failure to secure a job in Herbert's bank and thus escape from the decay of his own family. The severity of Quentin's reaction to Caddy's development finally drives him to suicide.

In so far as she creates this ripple of effect throughout her family, Caddy is placed firmly at the centre of the rest of the characters in the novel, but we should also remember that in *The Sound and the Fury* Faulkner only rarely comments directly upon his characters, and that his method of presenting them is very largely from the inside. We learn about them from their own words and from their memories of events and the words of others. We also learn about them from the ways in which they join together, or separate, or mix up their own memories and impressions of events and conversations. Because each of the brothers deals with the story and with each other in different ways, we are gradually able to piece together a full picture both of the story they are telling, and of themselves as characters within that story.

There is a total of sixty-four named characters in *The Sound and the Fury*. The following alphabetical list concentrates upon those who are most significant in the story.

Ames, Dalton: the man who first seduces Caddy Compson and who afterwards expresses concern for her welfare. He remains calm and controlled in the face of Quentin Compson's threat to kill him. Physically strong and widely travelled, Ames becomes in Quentin's mind a figure to be irrationally hated and envied.

Anse: marshal of a Cambridge suburb, who arrests Quentin after the episode with the little Italian girl.

Bascomb, Maury (Uncle Maury): Mrs Compson's brother, who does not work for a living, but instead borrows money from anyone who will lend it to him, including even the Negro servant Dilsey. He is a drunkard and a wastrel who pretends to be a Southern gentleman. Because of his illicit affair with Mrs Patterson he is punched and beaten by her husband.

Bland, Gerald: one of Quentin Compson's fellow students at Harvard University, who goes rowing in flannels and a stiff hat, attempting to copy his idea of students at the University of Oxford in England. At his mother's picnic he makes boastful remarks about his successes with women, for which Quentin attacks him and is beaten.

Bland, Mrs: wealthy, class-conscious mother of Gerald. She continually boasts about his qualities and achievements. Quentin considers her and Gerald to be vulgar, showy people who do not know how to live with their wealth.

Burgess: the Compson neighbour who hits Benjy with a fence-rail when Benjy frightens his daughter and some other girls who are returning from school.

Charlie: one of Caddy's boy friends who is seen by Benjy kissing her on a swing.

Compson, Benjamin (Benjy): the idiot, aged thirty-three, who is first named Maury after his mother's brother, but at his mother's insistence is later renamed Benjamin. He is the youngest of the Compson children and cannot talk, but has three ways of recording his emotions: by howling, by moaning, and by being quiet. Benjy loves three things: the pasture, his sister Caddy, and firelight. He is also comforted by mirrors, a cushion, and a slipper. Being an idiot, he cannot make judgements upon events, but simply tells us what happens and what he remembers, making no distinction between the two. Faulkner once said of Benjy that 'the only thing that held him into any sort of reality, into the world at all, was the trust that he had for his sister, that he knew that she loved him and would defend him, and so she was the whole world to him, and these things were flashes that were reflected on her as in a mirror'.* But Benjy is able to react to different kinds of things, whether a movement, an object or a sound such as hearing the golfers shout 'caddy'. These things serve as a kind of trigger which starts him remembering events, and he will then live through those events as though they were happening for the first time. Although he cannot make judgements upon events, Benjy does serve as an image of suffering innocence. And because he remains innocent throughout the story, he shows the reader how to react to other characters in the novel. If people treat Benjy kindly they are morally good, and the opposite is also true. In this way the passive character of Benjy becomes the most active moral guide for the reader's response to other characters.

Compson, Candace (Caddy): the only girl child in the Compson family, and the only one of the children not to have a narrative section in the novel, Caddy is a source of warmth and vitality. She enjoys and expresses love and so stands in marked contrast to her three brothers, and to the general mood of despair and decline in the novel. Faulkner himself saw Caddy as 'the beautiful one, she was my heart's darling'.† As a growing girl Caddy behaves naturally and spontaneously, but the extreme reactions of her family as she comes to maturity make her feel guilty and sinful. Her natural sexuality becomes promiscuous, but she loves her illegitimate daughter enough to place herself at Jason's mercy for her sake. Caddy is devoted to Benjy, and besides being able to understand Quentin better than he understands himself, she goes as far as offering herself to him in order to ease some of the pressures in his own mind. But she loves life too much actually to help Quentin in his proposed suicide pact. When she is about to leave the family as Herbert's wife, her major concern is still for the well-being of Quentin, Benjy and their father. At this stage her feelings of guilt are overpowering.

Compson, Caroline Bascomb (Mrs Compson): a mother of four children who is incapable of showing them any maternal affection, but instead pities herself and her reduced circumstances. She feels bitter that she can no longer live as she feels a Southern lady from the Bascomb family should, and spends much of her time in bed 'saving her strength' and being a burden to others. Beneath her complaints about her lot in life she is self-centred and ruthless. Her treatment of Dilsey is as hard-hearted and uncaring as her lack of feeling for her own children, and she shows herself capable of setting Jason to spy on Caddy and then laying the blame on Quentin. Her pretended preference for Jason is nothing other than thinly disguised self-interest since she depends upon him for her own survival.

*Faulkner in the University, pp.63–4.
†Faulkner in the University, p.6.

Compson, Jason, junior: the most vicious and self-centred character in *The Sound and the Fury*, and one of the most cruel and brutal ever created by Faulkner who considered that Jason 'represented complete evil'.* He cheats and steals from his own family, and, driven by a bitter spirit of revenge, he is without a single shred of decent feeling. In order to justify his failures he feeds on the hate which dominates his personality. He suffers from partial sexual impotence, and he uses cold and calculating logic as an excuse for his heartless behaviour. But in spite of his callous reasoning, Jason also behaves in ways that are as irrational as Benjy's or Quentin's behaviour. Instead of investing the one thousand dollars from his mother in the store where he works, and thus making himself a partner in the business, he buys a motor car which causes him intense physical pain through violent headaches. He needlessly upsets everyone around him, and the inner fury which drives him to pursue his niece Miss Quentin almost results in his own death. Many of his actions are marked by a similar lack of logic and reason.

Compson, Jason Richmond (Mr Compson): conscious that he is seeing the end of a once proud family, and feeling unable to do anything about it, Mr Compson is a defeated man who hides behind a philosophy which pretends to have no faith in anything. He appears to be wise and witty, but in fact his opinions are based upon hopelessness and despair. Although he makes occasional efforts to be a father to his children, he steadily drinks himself to death. In trying to pass on what he considers to be wisdom to Quentin, Mr Compson unwittingly contributes to his son's confusion by preventing him from developing his own view of life.

Compson, Quentin: the most complex character in the Compson family, Quentin is intelligent enough to understand what the family has been in the past, and too sensitive to cope with what it has become in the present. Heavily influenced by his father, who has taught him that 'all men are just . . . dolls stuffed with sawdust swept up from trash heaps', Quentin's narrative shows his father's words mingling with his own. This gives the reader the impression that Quentin is unable to separate himself either from his father's influence or from the influence of the past. As Faulkner remarked, 'the action as portrayed by Quentin was transmitted to him through his father . . . it was the basic failure Quentin inherited through his father, or beyond his father . . . something had happened somewhere between the first Compson and Quentin.'† We also know from Faulkner that Quentin 'loved not his sister's body but some concept of Compson honour', and partly because he feels that this honour is stained and cannot be rescued, Quentin commits suicide. We know, too, that Quentin was

Faulkner at Nagano, p.104.
†*Faulkner in the University*, pp.2–3.

not attracted to 'the idea of the incest he would not commit, but [to] some . . . concept of its eternal damnation'.* This helps to explain Quentin's obsession with time. A sense of the Southern past which claimed to be noble, courageous and honest presses in upon Quentin's sense of present deceit and dishonour. In addition to this, Quentin is frequently reminded of his own obvious inability to defend his sister's honour according to notions of chivalry and family pride. He is physically weak, and not a good horseman. His own virginity and dislike of female company contrast with Caddy's sexual vitality to place yet further strains upon his already unstable mind. He does not have the mental strength to survive.

Compson, Miss Quentin: Caddy's illegitimate daughter is treated cruelly by Jason and this has helped to make her rebellious and promiscuous. She is self-indulgent and is capable of being spiteful. But she also has some of her mother's high-spirited nature as we see in the episode where she and her lover escape from Jason by deflating the tyres of his motor car. She also has the courage to steal back the money that is rightfully hers. Her most marked difference from her mother Caddy, however, is seen in her treatment of Benjy with whom she does not even like to eat meals.

Compson, 'Damuddy': the grandmother of the Compson children whose death in 1898 figures so largely in their memories and recollections.

Deacon: the black porter at Harvard with whom Quentin becomes friendly, and to whom he intends to leave clothing after he commits suicide.

Earl: the owner of the store where Jason Compson works and who keeps him in employment for the sake of Mrs Compson whom Earl treats in the manner of a Southern gentleman. It is for Mrs Compson's sake that Earl protects Jason over his lie about the one thousand dollars given by her to Jason for him to buy a partnership in the store.

Frony: the married daughter of Dilsey and Roskus.

Gibson, Dilsey: the noblest character in *The Sound and the Fury*, Dilsey is a mother to the Compson children as well as to her own. She gives to the Compson family whatever sense of order it still possesses, and it is significant that she is the only character other than Caddy who can quieten Benjy simply by telling him to hush. She is not intimidated by Jason, and she is able to cope with Mrs Compson's intolerable treatment of her. Her claim towards the end of the novel, 'I seed de beginnin, en now I sees de endin', is true, and as a faithful servant during the long and painful history of the family's decline, she suffers hardship with dignity, and remains gentle in the face of cruelty. She can be amusing and witty in a resilient kind of way, and she is tough and

*See the Appendix.

patient. Faulkner later said that 'Dilsey is one of my own favourite characters because she is brave, courageous, generous, gentle, and honest'.*

Gibson, Roskus: Dilsey's husband, who suffers badly from rheumatism. He senses that no good will come from his association with the Compson family.

Gibson, T.P.: the son of Dilsey and Roskus, who looks after Benjy until Luster is old enough to take over.

Gibson, Versh: the eldest son of Dilsey and Roskus who looks after Benjy until replaced by T.P.

Hatcher, Louis: the Negro who teaches Caddy to drive a car and who goes possum-hunting with Quentin and Versh.

Head, Sydney Herbert: the eligible bachelor found by Mrs Compson as a husband for Caddy during their holiday at French Lick. He divorces Caddy, probably because of her illegitimate daughter. Wealthy and unscrupulous, Herbert flatters Mrs Compson's vanity, and has been found guilty of cheating, both at cards and at his mid-term examinations at Harvard University.

Julio: the brother of the little Italian girl Quentin meets on the day of his suicide. He accuses Quentin of assaulting his sister.

Lorraine: Jason's mistress, who lives in Memphis, who has to help Jason to make love to her. Jason remembers giving her forty dollars.

Luster: the son of Frony and grandson of Dilsey. He is mischievous and sometimes guilty of cruelty in his treatment of Benjy. But he was, in Faulkner's own words, 'not only capable of the complete care and security of an idiot twice his age and three times his size, but could keep him entertained'.†

Mackenzie, Shreve: the easy-going Canadian friend and fellow student of Quentin Compson at Harvard University.

Mink: the man who, on Jason Compson's instructions, drives the horse and carriage rapidly past Caddy so that she can catch the merest glimpse of her daughter Miss Quentin.

Natalie: the childhood playmate of the Compson children, remembered by Quentin because she was the closest he ever came to a sexual encounter with a girl.

Patterson: the justifiably jealous husband who blacks Maury Bascomb's eye and bloodies his mouth.

Patterson, Mrs: wife of the above, who has an affair with Maury.

Shegog, Reverend: the preacher from Saint Louis who delivers the Easter Sunday sermon in the Negro church. The power of his eloquence and the passionate conviction of his faith have a deep and significant effect upon Dilsey.

Writers at Work, pp.117–8.
†See the Appendix.

Spoade: a senior student at Harvard University who has never been known to arrive at lessons properly dressed. Friendly if rather crude, he jokingly calls Shreve Mackenzie Quentin's husband, because they are room-mates and because Quentin is not interested in girls.

Theme and unity

When he was talking about how he came to write *The Sound and the Fury*, Faulkner once said that 'It began with a mental picture. I didn't realise at the time that it was symbolical. The picture was of the muddy seat of a little girl's drawers in a pear tree, where she could see through a window where her grandmother's funeral was taking place and report what was happening to her brothers on the ground below'.* Just before Caddy climbs the tree, we read that 'a snake crawled out from under the house', and when she is in the tree she is caught by Dilsey, who says 'You, Satan', and tells her to climb down. Caddy simply wants to learn what is going on in the house, but we are reminded of the Tree of Knowledge in the mythical garden of Eden with which the Devil tempted Eve.

The significance of this image is developed as the story unfolds. Just as Caddy climbs the tree to learn for herself, so she tries to enjoy living her own life, and for Benjy her natural vitality smells like trees. But when Caddy is in the tree her muddy drawers are soaking into her, and when she grows older her bright hopes for happiness become similarly soiled. We can see that Caddy's climb into the tree marks the beginning of her move into a different kind of life where she will be compelled to leave her family behind her. Caddy's own encounter with the Tree of Knowledge enables us to read *The Sound and the Fury* as a modern version of man's fall from innocence into experience. And, recalling Faulkner's own opinion that the novel is 'a tragedy of two lost women: Caddy and her daughter',† Caddy's climb into the tree early in the story begins a process that continues until her daughter Miss Quentin climbs down the same tree towards the end of the novel in order to escape from the collapse of the Compson family.

This tragic sense of collapse is presented through the opposing forces of love for others and love of self. We have seen that Dilsey is the only character who is capable of caring for the Compson children and looking after the whole family. In her case the humanity which she shows throughout the novel is joined with the notion of Christian love. The peace and understanding which Dilsey discovers through the Reverend Shegog's sermon, even though it makes her weep, is a symbolic reward for her patient suffering and loving strength through-

Writers at Work, p.118.
†*Writers at Work*, p.117.

out the long years of the Compson decline. And although it would be wrong to describe *The Sound and the Fury* as a Christian novel, Faulkner does use other references to the Christian religion, and to rituals associated with that religion, in order to suggest the tragic fact that love is vanishing from the world of his novel.

The most immediate clue to this aspect of Faulkner's approach is that he sets the main action of his story on the three days of an Easter weekend. This reminder of Christ's death adds to our feelings for Benjy's suffering innocence. Benjy's thirty-third birthday falls on that weekend, and Christ was thirty-three when he died. The feelings of loving self-sacrifice and hope associated with the crucifixion and resurrection of Christ are betrayed by the behaviour of the Compson family. Furthermore, both Benjy and Quentin remember incidents from their past which happened at Christmas. Faulkner places Benjy's memories of Christmas at the very beginning of the story, and we can see that he has arranged the pattern of his novel so that in some ways it mirrors the Christian cycle from Christmas to Easter, from birth to death. The Reverend Shegog's sermon towards the end of the novel expresses the Christian hope of life after death.

A further way in which Faulkner links his story of lovelessness with the failure of Christian ideals is suggested by his use of water imagery in the novel. In Christian ritual water is the sign of baptism, the purifying of the soul, and the promise of everlasting life. In *The Sound and the Fury*, Caddy repeatedly tries, unsuccessfully, to wash away the feelings of guilt for sexual experience which her family makes her feel. Her brother Quentin commits suicide by drowning.

To account for the failure of love in the novel, Faulkner explores particular kinds of reason and intellect. Mr Compson builds a philosophy of weariness and despair behind which he can hide from the collapse of his family. But this reasoning is damaging to his sons and in the end it offers no protection for Mr Compson himself. He turns to alcohol as a means of escape. His son Quentin is obsessed both by his own feelings for his family and by the wider history of which his family forms a part. But although he thinks about the meaning of his own and his family's present condition, he is unable to reason a way out of his problems. He cannot bring his own feelings and desires face to face with circumstances which appear to him to be fixed on an unchangeable course.

In Jason Compson Faulkner presents a grasping and calculating system of values which might be described as the reasoning of ruthless self-interest. By cancelling out all feelings of the heart and by using only a thieving intellect, Jason simply tries to make for himself as much money as he can. Although he is defeated in these aims, he ends his narrative still hoping to win money back from the stock market. In some ways Jason appears as an extreme example of the faults of society at that time. His continued gambling on the stock market is one sign of this. Many of the townspeople of Jefferson are doing the same thing, and in 1929 this kind of wild gambling on an even wider scale brought about the collapse of the Wall Street stock market and the great economic depression of the 1930s.

Although *The Sound and the Fury* is a disturbing story of loss, collapse, and decay, it does not offer only a vision of despair and hopelessness. Faulkner's comment upon Caddy in the Appendix, 'Doomed and knew it, accepted the doom without either seeking or fleeing it', suggests that the Compsons' fate can be faced and accepted without despair. Although the Compson family has fallen into a state of disorder and chaos, the novelist has employed many different techniques to give the reader an inner sense of order which the Compson family can no longer see for itself. By these means Faulkner creates unity out of disunity and provides a sense of complete and ordered experience out of a series of disordered and incomplete pieces.

Caddy's love is at the heart of the novel, and Dilsey, too, is a loving and admirable character. The detailed attention which Faulkner pays to Dilsey's spiritual uplifting in the last section of the novel reminds us that in spite of all its anguish and pain, *The Sound and the Fury* is a novel about the enduring power of love. Faulkner believes that 'we must take the trouble and sin with us as we go, and we must cure that trouble and sin as we go'.*

If we remember these things and consider also the finally achieved sense of order in the novel, then we can more easily understand the optimism of Faulkner's Nobel Prize Address, in which he said:

I believe that man will not merely endure: he will prevail. He is immortal, not because he alone among creatures has an inexhaustible voice, but because he has a soul, a spirit capable of compassion and sacrifice and endurance. The poet's, the writer's duty is to write about these things. It is his privilege to help man endure by lifting his heart, by reminding him of the courage and honour and hope and pride and compassion and pity and sacrifice which have been the glory of his past. The poet's voice need not merely be the record of man, it can be one of the props, the pillars to help him endure and prevail.†

Faulkner at Nagano, p.77.
†Reprinted in *The Portable Faulkner*, edited by Malcolm Cowley, The Viking Press, New York, revised edition 1967, p.724.

Part 4

Hints for study

General: story and structure

These notes, and other critical texts such as those listed in Part 5, can help your study of *The Sound and the Fury*, reminding you of the story, of how it is told, and of the nature and significance of the whole novel. However, in studying literature, there is no substitute for a close, careful reading of the text, making sure you understand it for yourself.

This is particularly true of *The Sound and the Fury*. The greatest problem in studying this novel is the difficulty of working out the story itself, and of following what is supposed to be happening, especially in the first two sections. The best way to improve your knowledge of *The Sound and the Fury* is to read it again. Most readers find the novel very confusing when they read it for the first time. But if it is read a second time, when the reader is more familiar with the characters, and has worked out some of the story from the clearer last two sections, many of the confusing parts of the novel fall into place. Even the more difficult sections – 'April Seventh, 1928' and 'June Second, 1910' – begin to make sense and can be understood more easily. Rereading the novel is surprising and rewarding: *The Sound and the Fury* no longer seems only a confusing 'tale told by an idiot'. Instead, its meaning, pattern, and significance begin to be appreciated.

Even on a second reading, however, you may find that you are not able to follow every part of the first two sections. The summaries in Part 2 of these notes should be used to help. By sorting out all the episodes of *The Sound and the Fury*, and placing them in the order in which they happened, these summaries make the actual story of the Compson family clearer. If you are in doubt about any part of the novel, you should look back at Part 2. The first words of each part of 'April Seventh, 1928' and 'June Second, 1910' printed in normal or *italic* type are followed by a note of the episode in the Compson story to which that part refers. You should also use the index of characters on pp.70–5 if you are in doubt about any of the characters referred to in the text. The general summary at the start of Part 2, and the list on p.61 of the main events remembered by Benjy, can also be used as quick reminders of the Compson history.

However, it would be a great mistake to try to understand *The Sound and the Fury* entirely through the use of these summaries. They are not a substitute for the novel itself, as they do not present its whole feeling accurately. As Jean-Paul Sartre went on to suggest in his essay (quoted on p.56), if we read a summary of the novel arranged in the order of time, rather than in Faulkner's order, we are really reading a completely different story. Much of the meaning – and the uniqueness – of *The Sound and the Fury* depends not only on the Compson story itself, but on the way that story is told. Why is this tale partly told by an idiot? How did Faulkner 'break up the time of his story and scramble the pieces'? Why did he do so? What do we feel about the difficulty of the novel as we read it?

Most of these questions are partly answered in Part 3 of these notes, but you should ask and try to answer them for yourself as you reread the novel. Always remember to ask yourself not only *what* is going on, but *how* we are told about it, and *why* the novel is presented as it is. A good student of literature reads very thoroughly, and thinks very carefully about the nature and meaning of what she or he reads.

Characterisation

Most novels introduce us very carefully to characters, usually telling us something about their appearance, about what sort of person they are, what kind of things they do, and so on. In *The Sound and the Fury*, however, characters are not immediately presented to us in this way. Just as the story of the Compson family is told indirectly and out of order, so the nature of character is seldom stated directly. Instead, it is built up gradually by hints and impressions, which we must judge for ourselves. For example, we learn a great deal about Benjy and his mind from the first section of the novel, but it is not until the last section that we are told anything about his appearance – his 'pale blue eyes' and 'shambling gait like a trained bear'.

The same is true of most of the characters in *The Sound and the Fury*. From the workings of his mind on June Second, 1910, we find out a lot about Quentin Compson, but he is never presented directly, and Faulkner includes no comments of his own about his character. Instead, we build up an impression of Quentin not only from the second section of the novel, but also from the points of view of other characters: consider, for example, how Benjy remembers him as a child, what Jason thinks about him, how Caddy and Dalton Ames treat him, and so on. Strong feelings are built up even about the novel's lesser characters: think what an exact impression of Mrs Compson we have from her conversations and actions (for example, her treatment of Benjy, or of Dilsey) even before a clearer picture is reached in the last section of the novel.

In answering questions about a work of literature, it is not usually good enough to state only what you know about it. You must also explain how you learned what you did, and why you think as you do. So it is always useful to ask yourself at least two questions about each character: not only 'What do we know about him or her?' but also 'How do we know it?'. This is especially true of *The Sound and the Fury*, in which characters are presented indirectly and subtly. You should look back at the list of characters in Part 3, decide what you think about each of them, and work out how your opinion was formed.

In each case, ask yourself *how* the character was presented. Did we follow the workings of his mind? (Benjy, Quentin, and Jason.) Did the character appear as part of the memories of another character? (Caddy, Mr Compson, Mrs Compson.) If so, were they remembered by more than one character, and does this affect our feelings for them? (You might think of the differences between Benjy, Jason, and Quentin's memories of Mr Compson, or of Caddy, for example.) Does this character appear in the fourth section of the novel? If so, are they directly described or commented upon by the author? (Notice how much more we learn about Luster, Benjy, Mrs Compson, Jason and Dilsey in 'April Sixth, 1928'.) Make sure you know something about each character, and can also explain how you learned what you did.

Style and technique

Faulkner's statement quoted on p.62 suggests that he tried four different ways of writing *The Sound and the Fury*, and this partly accounts for the difference in styles between the sections of the novel. If necessary, remind yourself of the nature of each by referring back to the notes (pp.63–8) in Part 3. The easiest way to remember the differences between the sections is to think of the characters whose thoughts are presented in the first three; and to remember that the fourth section is written directly from the author's own point of view. Benjy is an idiot, with a child-like mind; Quentin is intelligent but mentally disturbed; Jason is very bitter but largely sane; and the author, of course, looks clearly and objectively at the events he describes. The differences between the minds of each character account for the differences in style and language between the first three sections, and Faulkner, 'gathering the pieces together', gives order and clarity to the fourth.

You should look back over the novel, reminding yourself of the nature of each section. You should also notice Faulkner's use of Southern Negro dialect, find examples of this, and be able to say how and why it is used (see p.68).

Specimen questions

To help you to think about *The Sound and the Fury*, here are some typical questions about it. They should help you to decide what to look for in going back over the novel. Try to answer each of them for yourself – at least make some notes – before you look at the brief outline answer which follows. The questions are roughly arranged in order of increasing difficulty: the first five test your knowledge and memory of the novel; the rest question more generally your understanding and appreciation of it.

---

(1) *Write notes on the following characters: Uncle Maury, Miss Quentin, Mrs Compson, Gerald Bland*

See 'Characterisation' in Parts 3 and 4.

---

(2) *How does Luster look after Benjy on April Seventh, 1928?*

See Part 2 for a summary of Benjy's day. Note the various ways Luster amuses Benjy and tries to keep him quiet. He lets him watch the golfers, play in the stream and in his 'graveyard', and so on. Although he does not often understand the reasons for Benjy's bellowing, he always tries to find a way of quietening him, often by giving him flowers to hold. Sometimes, he does not succeed in controlling him: for example, when Benjy disturbs Miss Quentin in the swing. As the day goes on, Luster loses his patience, perhaps because he is worried about his lost quarter. Eventually, he teases Benjy deliberately, and is scolded by Dilsey, especially after Benjy burns his hand.

---

(3) *Write an account of Quentin's last day at Harvard*

Like question 2, this asks for straightforward description. See Part 2 for a summary of Quentin's day. Note the way his thoughts and memories become increasingly confused with what is actually happening to him.

---

(4) *Describe Jason's treatment of Miss Quentin as it is presented in 'April Sixth, 1928'*

See the summary of 'April Sixth, 1928' in Part 2. You should mention that we learn a great deal about Jason's cruel and unloving character from the unpleasant way he treats his niece.

---

(5) *Write an account of Dilsey's visit to the Negro church on Easter Sunday*

This episode is also summarised in Part 2. But as well as giving details of what actually happens, you should examine the significance of this visit. How does it affect Dilsey and Benjy, and what do their responses tell us? How does their visit relate to the treatment of religion in the novel? What is the significance of the sermon preached by the Reverend Shegog? What do we learn about Dilsey and her relation to the Compsons?

---

(6) *Faulkner once called Jason 'the first sane Compson'. Do you think this description is correct?*

See 'Characterisation' in Part 3, and look again at the last two sections of the novel. Jason seems to live very exactly, always noting the time, the amount of money he spends, the state of the cotton market, and so on. He certainly thinks that he always behaves and acts in a sane way. But perhaps he is less sensible than he thinks. Do all his actions seem reasonable? Why does he chase Miss Quentin? Why should a man who suffers from the smell of petrol buy a car? Why is he so nasty to his boss, Earl? At any rate, even if Jason can be called sane, his sanity is much less pleasant than Benjy's or Quentin's madness.

---

(7) *Choose one character from* The Sound and the Fury *and discuss the effect their childhood and upbringing had on them*

In answering this question, you could write about any of the Compson children, or about Miss Quentin. For example, you might think about Benjy's happy memories of his childhood, and how things happened to change his secure picture of his family. Or you might consider Quentin's feelings for his sister, and what he learned from his father, and what he thought of his weak mother. You might look at the way Miss Quentin grows up in a 'home' run mostly by Jason and Mrs Compson. In any case, you should choose a character you know well and can write about thoroughly; then think about the incidents that took place as they grew up, and how these might have affected them.

---

(8) *Shortly before her wedding, Quentin blames Caddy for the unpleasant circumstances of the Compson family. Do you think this accusation is fair?*

At the time of Caddy's wedding, Quentin is perhaps exaggerating. As time goes on, however, it does seem that Caddy's actions bring about several of the disasters in her family: Quentin's suicide, or her father's death from drink, for example. But Caddy herself always acts with love and affection: her tragedy is that her family cannot respond normally to her, but are constantly upset by her actions. Although Quentin commits suicide largely because of the loss of his sister, his death results at least as much from the strange nature of his own mind as through any real fault of Caddy's. A good answer should consider both sides of the question: both Caddy's partial responsibility, and her partial innocence.

(9) *How is Dilsey presented in* The Sound and the Fury?

Dilsey is the most admirable character in *The Sound and the Fury*. Note what a clear feeling of her strength and endurance is developed even before we see her directly in the fourth section, and consider her significance for the novel as a whole (see 'Theme and unity' in Part 3).

(10) *Compare and contrast the ways we are shown the operations of the minds of Benjy and Quentin*

See Part 3, generally, but especially 'Style and technique'.

(11) *What features of* The Sound and the Fury *make it a difficult novel to read?*

See Part 3, 'The novelist against time'.

(12) *Should Faulkner have chosen a simpler technique in writing the story of the Compson family?*

See Part 3, 'Introduction: the novelist against time'; 'Structure'; and 'Theme and unity'.

Part 5

Suggestions for further reading

The text

The text used in these notes is the Penguin paperback edition of *The Sound and the Fury*, Penguin Books, Harmondsworth, 1964, and reprinted. Since there are several current American editions of *The Sound and the Fury*, with differently numbered pages, no reference to page numbers has been made.

Faulkner's other works

Faulkner's varied creative energy produced a literary output of an extent unusual among American novelists. He published eighteen novels: *Soldier's Pay* (1926), *Mosquitoes* (1927), *Sartoris* (1929), *The Sound and the Fury* (1929), *As I Lay Dying* (1930), *Sanctuary* (1931), *Light in August* (1932), *Pylon* (1935), *Absalom, Absalom!* (1936), *The Unvanquished* (1938), *The Wild Palms* (1939), *The Hamlet* (1940), *Go Down, Moses* (1942), *Intruder in the Dust* (1948), *A Fable* (1954), *The Town* (1957), *The Mansion* (1959) and *The Reivers* (1962). The dates refer to the first American editions; these were usually quickly followed by English editions. Most of the novels are available in cheap modern editions: many appear in Penguin editions, for example.

Faulkner's many short stories appear in a one-volume edition, *Collected Short Stories,* Chatto and Windus, London, 1951.

Although Faulkner is not particularly respected as a poet, his verse forms an interesting part of his early career. A good collection is *The Marble Faun and A Green Bough*, Random House, New York, 1960, first published as separate volumes in 1924 and 1933 respectively.

Mention must be made of another collection of Faulkner's work: *The Portable Faulkner,* ed. Malcolm Cowley, Viking Press, New York, 1946; also available in many cheap current editions, including Penguin. In editing this volume, Cowley selected some of Faulkner's short stories and pieces of his novels and put them together to give a complete history of Faulkner's South. The result is a very good selection of some of the best of his work, which also gives a clear idea of his whole literary output. Faulkner himself remarked of Cowley's work in producing this volume 'The job is splendid', and added that he could not have done it better himself. Most usefully, too, *The Portable Faulkner* contains the Appendix Faulkner wrote to make the history of the Compson family clearer. Although this Appendix is not really part of *The Sound and the Fury*, it is a fascinating account of Faulkner's own thoughts about his characters, and can add greatly to our understanding of the novel.

Although Faulkner did not wish his correspondence to be made public, his letters have been published recently, in *Selected Letters of William Faulkner*, ed. Joseph L. Blotner, Random House, New York, 1977. Some very revealing comments on *The Sound and the Fury* appear between pages 41 and 44 of this volume.

Some of Faulkner's speeches and other public writings have been collected in *Essays, Speeches and Public Letters by William Faulkner*, ed. James B. Meriwether, Random House, New York, 1965; and Chatto and Windus, London 1967. This volume contains 'Mississippi', a statement of Faulkner's feelings for the South.

Biographies and critical studies can be helpful, but one of the best ways to learn more about an author is to read more of what he wrote himself. Faulkner's characters often appear in more than one novel. Members of the Compson family, for example, reappear in the short stories 'A Justice', 'That Evening Sun', and 'Lion'; and in the novels *The Town, The Mansion*, and *Absalom, Absalom!* The early short story 'The Kingdom of Heaven' is also relevant to a study of *The Sound and the Fury*. Mention of the Compsons in these other works is often made only in passing, but can sometimes be usefully related to *The Sound and the Fury*. Along with *The Sound and the Fury, As I Lay Dying* and *Light in August* are often said to be Faulkner's best novels, and anyone wishing to read further might well start there. *As I Lay Dying* shows the same sort of brilliance and difficulty of technique as *The Sound and the Fury*; *Light in August* is more straightforward.

Biographical

BLOTNER, JOSEPH L.: *William Faulkner: A Biography*, 2 vols., Chatto and Windus, London, 1974; and Random House, New York, 1974. The standard biography, a very long and detailed work. Unless the reader wishes to follow Faulkner's life particularly closely, one of the shorter accounts of his career given in critical works should give enough information.

COUGHLAN, ROBERT: *The Private World of William Faulkner*, Harper and Brothers, New York, 1953. A shorter, less scholarly account of the life of Faulkner and his family. It includes several photographs of the novelist and a number of amusing anecdotes.

Towards the end of his life, Faulkner spent some time as a writer in residence at the University of Virginia. While there, he recorded several interviews, and these have since been published in *Faulkner in the University*: Class Conferences at the University of Virginia, 1957–8, ed. Joseph L. Blotner and F.L. Gwynn, The University of Virginia Press, Charlottesville, 1959. Several revealing comments on *The Sound and the Fury*, and Faulkner's fiction in general, appear in this volume.

Criticism

If you are an advanced student, it may be useful to look at one or two of the following books. If you are not an advanced student, the first and second will be of most use to you.

MILLGATE, MICHAEL: *William Faulkner*, Writers and Critics Series, Oliver and Boyd, Edinburgh and London, 1961. A simple and straightforward introduction to Faulkner the novelist.

VOLPE, EDMOND L.: *A Reader's Guide to William Faulkner*, Thames and Hudson, London, 1964. A most useful study, both as a general introduction to Faulkner and as an explanation and clarification of some of the difficulties of *The Sound and the Fury*.

WARREN, ROBERT PENN (ED.): *Twentieth Century Views of Faulkner*, Prentice-Hall, New Jersey, 1966. Short critical essays on Faulkner's fiction generally. There are several on *The Sound and the Fury*, including those by Jean-Paul Sartre and Michael Millgate (see below).

COWAN, M.H. (ED.): *Twentieth Century Interpretations of The Sound and the Fury*, Prentice-Hall, New Jersey, 1968. A collection of critical essays.

BACKMANN, MELVIN: *Faulkner: The Major Years*, Indiana University Press, Bloomington, 1966. Contains a good chapter on *The Sound and the Fury*, particularly enlightening about the novel's symbolism.

BROOKS, CLEANTH: *William Faulkner: The Yoknapatawpha Country*, Yale University Press, New Haven, 1963. Includes an excellent chapter on *The Sound and the Fury*.

HOFFMANN, FREDERICK J., AND VICKERY, OLGA W. (EDS.): *William Faulkner: Three Decades of Criticism*, Michigan State College Press, East Lansing, 1960. A collection of critical essays on Faulkner's novels, including several on *The Sound and the Fury*.

MILLGATE, MICHAEL: *The Achievement of William Faulkner*, Constable, London, 1964. Contains a detailed biographical introduction. The chapter on *The Sound and the Fury* is reprinted in the work by R.P. Warren listed above.

SWIGGART, PETER: *The Art of Faulkner's Novels*, University of Texas Press, Austin, 1962. Contains a good chapter on *The Sound and the Fury*.

THOMPSON, LAWRANCE: *William Faulkner: An Introduction and Interpretation*, Barnes and Noble, New York, 1963. A complicated but excellent chapter on Faulkner's technique in *The Sound and the Fury*.

VICKERY, OLGA: *The Novels of William Faulkner*, Louisiana State University Press, Louisiana, 1959. Includes a very intelligent and thorough analysis of *The Sound and the Fury*.

The authors of these notes

Colin Nicholson lectures in English and North American literature at Edinburgh University. He is co-editor of *Tropic Crucible: Self and Theory in Language and Literature* and of *Canadian Story and History 1885–1985*. He also edited *Alexander Pope: Essays for the Tercentenary*.

Randall Stevenson was educated in Glasgow and at the Universities of Edinburgh and Oxford. After teaching for a year in North-West Nigeria, he returned to Edinburgh University where he has been a lecturer in English Literature since 1978. He was also a Director of the Scottish Universities' International Summer School in 1981 and 1982, and has lectured for the British Council in Bulgaria, Poland, Portugal and Yugoslavia. He is the author of York Notes on *David Copperfield* and, with Colin Nicholson, of *The Crying of Lot 49*. His other publications include *The British Novel since the Thirties* (1986) and *The British Novel in the Twentieth Century: An Introductory Bibliography* (1988).